JOSEPH CONRAD lived a life that was as fantastic as any of his fiction. Born in Poland, December 3, 1857, he died in England on August 3, 1924. This native of an inland country spent his youth at sea, and although relatively ignorant of the English language until age twenty, he ultimately became one of the greatest of English novelists and stylists. Conrad's parents were aristocrats, ardent patriots who died when he was a child as a result of their revolutionary activities. He went to sea at sixteen, taught himself English, and after diligent study gradually worked his way up until he passed his master's examination and was given command of merchant ships in the Orient and on the Congo. At the age of thirty-two he decided to try his hand at writing, left the sea, married, and became the father of two sons. Although his work won the admiration of critics, sales were small, and debts and poor health plagued Conrad for many years. He was a nervous, introverted, gloomy man for whom writing was an agony, but he was rich in friends who appreciated his genius, among them Henry James, Stephen Crane, and Ford Madox Ford. Among his best-known works are *Aylmayer's Folly* (1895), *The Nigger of the "Narcissus"* (1897), *Lord Jim* (1900), *Heart of Darkness* (1902), *The Secret Sharer* (1907), *Chance* (1913), and *Victory* (1915).

JOYCE CAROL OATES is the author of 27 novels and numerous collections of stories, poetry, and plays. The Roger S. Berlind Distinguished Professor in the Humanities at Princeton University, she won the National Book Award and has been nominated for a Pulitzer prize. In 1996 she received the PEN–Bernard Malamud Award for the short story.

JOSEPH CONRAD

Heart of Darkness
and
The Secret Sharer

With a New Introduction by
Joyce Carol Oates

A SIGNET CLASSIC

SIGNET CLASSIC
Published by New American Library, a division of
Penguin Group (USA) Inc., 375 Hudson Street,
New York, New York 10014, U.S.A.
Penguin Books Ltd, 80 Strand,
London WC2R 0RL, England
Penguin Books Australia Ltd, 250 Camberwell Road,
Camberwell, Victoria 3124, Australia
Penguin Books Canada Ltd, 10 Alcorn Avenue,
Toronto, Ontario, Canada M4V 3B2
Penguin Books (NZ), cnr Airborne and Rosedale Roads,
Albany, Auckland 1310, New Zealand

Penguin Books Ltd, Registered Offices:
80 Strand, London WC2R 0RL, England

Published by Signet Classic, an imprint of New American Library,
a division of Penguin Group (USA) Inc.

First Signet Classic Printing, December 1950
First Signet Classic Printing (Oates Introduction), September 1997
20 19 18 17 16

Introduction copyright © The Ontario Review, Inc., 1997
All rights reserved

 REGISTERED TRADEMARK—MARCA REGISTRADA

Library of Congress Catalog Card Number: 97-66757

Printed in the United States of America

CONTENTS

v

Introduction
by Joyce Carol Oates

> My task which I am trying to achieve is, by the
> power of the written word, to make you hear, to
> make you feel—it is, before all, to make you *see*.
> —Joseph Conrad,
> Preface, *The Nigger of the "Narcissus,"*
> 1897

Like those other masterworks of the English fin de
siècle, Robert Louis Stevenson's *Dr. Jekyll and Mr.
Hyde* (1886), Oscar Wilde's *The Picture of Dorian
Gray* (1890–91), and Henry James's *The Turn of the
Screw* (1898), to which it bears a subtle thematic kinship, Joseph Conrad's "Heart of Darkness" (1902) is
a work of the imagination that has transcended its
late-Victorian era to acquire the stature, with the passing of time, of one of the great visionary self-examina-
tions of Western civilization. Based, like most of
Conrad's fiction, upon personal experience, "Heart of
Darkness" is a rare Symbolist work with roots in historic authenticity; its theme is nothing less than the
acknowledgment of a tragic darkness—the ethic of the
"brute"—in the heart of late-nineteenth-century
Christian-capitalist Europe. Out of his outraged wit-
nessing of what he called "the vilest scramble for loot
that ever disfigured the history of human conscious-
ness"—the plunder of Africa by Europe—Conrad created a universal parable of man's fallen nature in the
guise of an adventure/mystery tale.

In *Dr. Jekyll and Mr. Hyde,* Robert Louis Stevenson
created a vivid, iconic metaphor for civilized man's
divided nature: there is the "good" if passionless Dr.

Jekyll, and there is his suppressed brother self, the stunted, impassioned, "evil" Hyde who dwells within Jekyll and can be released—fatally—by a magic elixir. In Oscar Wilde's *The Picture of Dorian Gray,* the seductively beautiful young Dorian commits sins against humanity that are engraved, not on his unblemished, never-aging face, but on the face of his portrait, which has been hidden away: what more striking metaphor for the hypocritical nature of privileged Caucasian bourgeois society? In Henry James's enigmatic *The Turn of the Screw,* that most elegantly constructed of ghost stories, the reader is confronted by a seemingly good Christian governess who may herself be the catalyst of the destruction of her young charges: Does this zealous, well-intentioned young woman discover perversity and evil surrounding her, or is she luridly imagining it? Joseph Conrad's "Heart of Darkness," though elaborately composed of oscillating images of light and dark, order and chaos, is by far the most realistic of these unusual works of fiction; yet here, too, is a powerful mythic portrait of a "good" man, Kurtz (the chief of the inner station of the trading company, "an emissary of pity, and science, and progress, and devil knows what else"), who is simultaneously an "evil" man (a vicious, unscrupulous trader in ivory who ends up tyrannizing African natives, his jungle sanctuary surrounded by the grisly emblems of his madness, the decapitated heads of native "enemies"). Kurtz, whom Marlow had sought avidly, risking his own life in a treacherous and foolhardy adventure that comes close to destroying him, is both Dr. Jekyll and Mr. Hyde; the elixir that fatally releases his primitive, evil self is simply distance from home, the freedom of a white man's power over those whom he considers his racial "inferiors," whose influence over him is subliminal and unacknowledged:

> I tried to break the spell [Marlow says]—the heavy, mute spell of the wilderness—that seemed to draw him to its pitiless breast by the awakening of forgotten and brutal instincts, by the memory of gratified and

monstrous passions. This alone, I was convinced, had
driven him out to the edge of the forest, to the bush,
toward the gleam of fires, the throb of drums, the
drone of weird incantations. . . . There was nothing
either above or below him, and I knew it. He had
kicked himself loose of the earth. . . . His soul was
mad. Being alone in the wilderness, it had looked
within itself, and, by heavens! I tell you, it had gone
mad.

It is Marlow's compelling argument, and through
Marlow, Conrad's, that the mind of man is capable of
anything "because everything is in it, all the past as
well as all the future." Marlow's (and Conrad's) journey up the Congo is, in one sense, a journey back
into time: beginning with Marlow's apprehension that
England, too, was once "one of the dark places of the
earth" and moving to a consideration of the "fascination of the abomination"—the fascination of civilized
man for his primitive, atavistic roots. What romance
there is in Conrad's prose, in his celebration of such
truths: "The voice of the surf heard now and then was
a positive pleasure, like the speech of a brother." And
in the memorable passage in which Marlow describes
his excitement at setting out, at last, to meet the mysterious chief of the inner station, Kurtz:

> Going up that river was like traveling back to the
> earliest beginnings of the world, when vegetation ri-
> oted on the earth and the big trees were kings. An
> empty stream, a great silence, an impenetrable forest.
> The air was warm, thick, heavy, sluggish. There was
> no joy in the brilliance of sunshine. . . . You lost your
> way on that river as you would in a desert . . . till you
> thought yourself bewitched and cut off forever from
> everything you had known once—somewhere—far
> away—in another existence perhaps.

The anxieties aroused by Charles Darwin's controversial, bitterly contested theory of evolution by way
of natural selection, first promulgated in *Origin of Species* (1859) and subsequently in *The Descent of Man*

(1871) are given tragic dramatic form in the tale of
Kurtz's deterioration in the jungle, the much-acclaimed
Kurtz of whom it is said by Marlow that "all of Europe .had gone into [his] making." Conrad's irony is
a constant throughout the narrative, like a haunting
vibration beyond the sounds of words normally uttered. And what intransigent irony in Kurtz's final
words, as if Shakespeare's unregenerate Edmund, or
Iago, and not Lear or Othello, were the touchstones
of moral truth. Dying of fever in the jungle, as Marlow
nearly dies, Kurtz's famous pronouncement of his own
spiritual condition—"The horror! The horror!"—is a
judgment upon man's universal propensity for evil.
What is this mysterious kinship that Marlow feels with
the doomed man, whom he has traveled hundreds of
miles to meet, only to discover him moribund, hid-
eous? "It was as if an animated image of death carved
out of old ivory had been shaking its hand with menaces at a motionless crowd of men made of dark and
glittering bronze." (Compare Marlow's subterranean
connection with Kurtz to the idealized and romanti-
cized connection between the immature young captain
of "The Secret Sharer" and his double, the fugitive
Leggatt.) Yet, in his symbolic role as chief of the cov-
eted inner station, Kurtz is indeed, as Marlow claims,
a remarkable man:

> His stare . . . was wide enough to embrace the whole
> universe, piercing enough to penetrate all the hearts
> that beat in the darkness. He had summed up—he had
> judged. "The horror!" . . . It was an affirmation, a
> moral victory paid for by innumerable defeats, by
> abominable terrors, by abominable satisfactions. But
> it was a victory! That is why I have remained loyal to
> Kurtz to the last

(Kurtz's real-life model was a man named Georges
Antoine Klein, an employee of the Brussels-based
trading company Société Anonyme Belge pour le
Commerce du Haut-Congo, whom Conrad met shortly

before Klein's death. His body was buried at Tchumb-
iri on the Congo.)

Through the prism of shimmering, musical language
that is the essence of Conrad's achievement in "Heart
of Darkness," the author has hoped to elevate Kurtz,
a white racist murderer whose actions have parodied
the idealism of his speech, to the stature of tragedy;
he is one whose degradation at the end of his life can't
be the sole measure of his moral worth.

Like Herman Melville, who also went to sea as a
very young man, Joseph Conrad acquired in his early,
impressionistic years a rich store of material to be
transformed into tales and novels of exoticism, danger,
and rites of passage. Born Józef Teodor Konrad Kor-
zeniowski at Berdyczow in Podolia, Poland, on December 3, 1857, Conrad lost his parents at a young
age, attended school in Cracow, and first went to sea,
on a French merchant marine vessel, at the age of
seventeen. He is said to have attempted suicide at the
age of twenty-one, but recovered quickly and signed
on with the British merchant navy for whom he would
serve, at various ranks, for the next sixteen years. He
became a naturalized British subject in 1886 and
changed his name to Joseph Conrad; in that year he
wrote his first short story, "The Black Mate." His numerous voyages took him virtually everywhere—to the
West Indies, to Constaninople, to Sumatra, India,
Java, Australia, Singapore; most famously, and almost
fatally, to the Belgian Congo in 1890. Though desperate to earn a living, the youthful Conrad was clearly
a romantic for whom sailing was an emotional, perhaps even a spiritual vocation. Surely this is Conrad
speaking in the voice of Marlow, confiding in his fellow seafarers at the outset of "Heart of Darkness":

Now when I was a little chap I had a passion for maps.
I would look for hours at South America, or Africa,
or Australia, and lose myself in the glories of exploration. At that time there were many blank spaces on
the earth, and when I saw one that looked particularly

inviting on a map (but they all look that) I would
put my finger on it and say, "When I grow up, I will
go there."

By the time Marlow had grown up, however, Africa
had "ceased to be a blank space of delightful
mystery. . . . It had become a place of darkness. But
there was in it one river especially . . . resembling an
immense snake uncoiled, with its head in the sea, its
body at rest curving afar over a vast country, and its
tail lost in the depths of the land." This great river, the
Congo, fascinates Marlow "as a snake would a bird."

In June 1890, Conrad was appointed captain of a
river steamer on the Congo; ominously, his predecessor had been butchered by native Africans and his
body left to rot unburied in the jungle. Conrad's difficult four-mouth adventure, recorded more or less
faithfully in "Heart of Darkness," left him near death,
devastated with dysentery and fever; his health was
broken for the remainder of his life. Conrad's predi-
lection for extreme pessimism, depression, and anxiety
would seem to have been exacerbated by his physical
condition. In May 1891, for instance, following his return in Europe, he confided in a letter to a friend, "I
am still plunged in deepest night, and my dreams are
only nightmares." (See *Conrad* by Norman Sherry,
Thames & Hudson, 1972.)

Yet the experience was transforming to Conrad,
comparable to the experience of writers who have
seen armed combat firsthand cr have been wounded
in battle, for Conrad would one day claim that "before
the Congo, I was just an animal." By the end of 1894,
Conrad had retired from seafaring; his first novel, *Almayer's Folly,* was published and well received in
1895. His remarkable career had begun.

Though always a controversial figure, criticized in
some quarters for his intensely poetic, frequently rhe-
torical prose and for the unremitting pessimism of certain of his works, Conrad is generally acclaimed as
one of the progenitors, along with his mentors Gus-
tave Flaubert and Henry James, of the Modernist

novel; he has been called a master of the psychological novel, the political novel, and the "intellectual mystery" novel; the fastidiously rendered prose of such works as *The Nigger of the "Narcissus," "Heart of Darkness"* and *Nostromo,* among others, identifies him as a writer for whom language is a kind of music, rendered with a poet's ear. Following Henry James's example in his essay "The Art of Fiction" (1888), Conrad set out, in his Preface to *The Nigger of the "Narcissus"* (1897), to establish his belief in the alliance in prose fiction of the moral and the aesthetic; his elevation of the writing life is extreme, suggesting almost a religious, or mystical, vocation; the artist is one who snatches "in a moment of courage . . . a passing phase of life" in the effort of showing life's "vibration, its color, its form; and through its movement, its form, and its color, revel[s] the substance of its truth."

By the time of Conrad's death in 1924, in Canterbury, England, this Polish-born emigrant for whom English was not his first or even his second language, would be celebrated as one of the greatest of English novelists, revered as a classic in his own time.

Since its initial publication in 1902, in the volume *Youth,* Conrad's most meticulously poetic work of fiction, "Heart of Darkness," has acquired an extraordinary reputation. Nine decades after its publication it remains one of the most read, and debated, of English works of fiction; it was the model, in spirit, of the flawed but enormously ambitious film by Francis Ford Coppola, *Apocalypse Now** (1979); it has easily become the surpassing masterwork of Conrad's distinguished career, displacing even *The Nigger of the "Narcissus," Lord Jim* (1900), *Nostromo* (1904), *The*

---

*Coppola transformed "Heart of Darkness" into a grotesque melodrama set in Vietnam in the waning years of the Vietnam War. In the role of Marlow, an American army officer is sent to Cambodia to assassinate a renegade Green Beret colonel who has set himself up, like Kurtz, as a murderous madman-god. Imaginative in concept and vivid in execution, *Apocalypse Now* is undermined by the ludicrous overacting of Marlon Brando in the role of Kurtz, which neither he nor his director seems to have understood.

Secret Agent (1907), *Victory* (1915), and such brilliantly realized tales as "The Secret Sharer" and "An Outpost of Progress." Part of this is due, of course, to the novella's brevity; like Henry James's *The Turn of the Screw,* it is a feat of dramatic compression in which virtually every passage, if not every sentence, moves us ineluctably toward our moment of revelation: the unmasking of Kurtz, and his twin, terrible pronouncements, "Exterminate all the brutes!" and "The horror! The horror!" (The latter has achieved a kind of transcultural autonomy, very like Edvard Munch's 1895 woodcut "The Scream"—a bleakly comic shorthand for twentieth-century angst.)

Unlike other, longer works of Conrad's that provide the reader with imbricated layers of exposition, history, psychology, and description, "Heart of Darkness" moves swiftly forward as Marlow's journey moves him, by starts and stops, forward; this is an adventure/mystery story set in the most exotic of locales and fueled by a nightmare logic. The reader is meant to replicate Marlow's voyage as he journeys up the Congo in a snakelike passage into the depths of a formerly blank, unmapped territory: the human soul.

In recent years, Joseph Conrad's work, or more specifically, ideas of gender, race, class, and hegemony implicit in his work, have been severely criticized. The assumptions of Caucasian male privilege are no longer taken for granted among many readers. It should be acknowledged by Conrad's admirers that the audience for whom he imagined his work was almost exclusively male, and assuredly Caucasian. To readers not in this category, the occasionally dogmatic and even derisive nature of certain of Marlow's remarks will strike a discordant note:

> It's queer how out of touch with truth women are. They live in a world of their own, and there never has been anything like it, and never can be. It is too beautiful altogether, and if they were to set it up it would go to pieces before the first sunset. Some confounded fact we men have been living contentedly with ever

since the day of creation would start up and knock the whole thing over.

Leaving aside for the moment the improbability of an entire sex, and that the child-bearing sex, being permanently "out of touch with truth," we might assume, for argument's sake, that Marlow is speaking critically of a financially well-off, minimally educated class of women who, being denied the possibility of careers and any measure of autonomy apart from fathers, husbands, brothers, or sons, were kept in a perpetual state of childish dependence upon men—the "fact"-bearing sex. In the gothic-melodramatic final scene of Marlow's tale, in which he visits Kurtz's fiancée, the very emblem of Victorian moral hypocrisy and delusion, Conrad's misogyny is disguised by an air of pity and condescension; a full year after Kurtz's ignoble death, his intended is still in mourning, a neurasthenic apparition in black, with "a pale head, floating towards me in the dusk. . . . She carried her sorrowful head as if she were proud of that sorrow." The valiant Marlow, who detests lies, for lies are "tainted with death," nonetheless "laid the ghosts of [Kurtz's] gifts at last with a lie" by telling Kurtz's intended that, at the end of Kurtz's life, it was her name he uttered. (In fact, ironically, Kurtz's last words were "The horror! The horror!") Men must lie to women, Conrad argues, to preserve women's childlike state of delusion. In Conrad's ranked moral universe, men of a certain class are custodians of truth, facts, ideas, and the respect for tradition outlined in the British Navy handbook *An Inquiry into Some Points of Seamanship*; women are associated with lies, subterfuge, hypocrisy. (Caucasian women, that is. For a portrait of a black woman, consider Marlow's description of Kurtz's native mistress, of whom Marlow speaks awkwardly as "barbarous"—"savage and superb, wild-eyed and magnificent"—with a face that communicates a "tragic and fierce aspect of wild sorrow and of dumb pain mingled with the fear of some struggling, half-shaped resolve"—"like the wilderness itself, with an air of

brooding over an inscrutable purpose." Words piled
upon words, suggesting a generalized allegorical figure, a carved wooden sculpture symbolizing African
Woman, and not a living, breathing individual woman
who is supposed to be passionately in love with the
dying Kurtz.)

Conrad has been criticized more sharply for his pre-
sentations of men and women of color. Consider Marlow's astonishment and amusement when a black
African emulates "white" behavior:

> I had to look after the savage who was fireman. He
> was an improved specimen; he could fire up a vertical
> boiler. . . . To look at him was as edifying a sight as
> seeing a dog in a parody of breeches and a feather
> hat, walking on his hind-legs. . . . He had filed teeth,
> too, the poor devil, and the wool of his pate shaved
> into queer patterns, and three ornamental scars on
> each of his cheeks. He ought to have been clapping
> his hands and stamping his feet on the bank, instead
> of which he was hard at work, a thrall to strange
> witchcraft.

Elsewhere, African natives are "dusty niggers," "surly
niggers," "cannibals." Conrad, the moralist, the artist
for whom prose fiction is a vocation like the priest-
hood, painfully reveals himself in such passages, and
numerous others, as an unquestioning heir of centuries
of Caucasian bigotry. Yet it might be argued that Marlow, for all his condescension, represents a degree of
humanity not found in the other Caucasian Europeans
who are intent upon wresting from black Africa all
they can get. Marlow isn't in the Congo for ivory, or
money, or to advance his career; he takes on the cap-
taincy of the steamboat for adventure's sake, and becomes fascinated with the demonic figure of Kurtz, the
very embodiment of European civilization. Marlow's
sharp, cinematic eye brings alive for us these suffering
black men, whose plight is meant to move the hearts
of Conrad's educated, well-to-do English readers:

> Six black men advanced in a file, toiling up the

path. . . . I could see every rib, the joints of their limbs were like knots in a rope; each had an iron collar on his neck, and all were connected together with a chain whose bights swung between them, rhythmically clinking. . . . These men could by no stretch of imagination be called enemies. They were called criminals. . . . They passed me within six inches, without a glance, with that complete, deathlike indifference of unhappy savages.

Other black men, enslaved and driven like animals until they are of no further use, are allowed to crawl off and die. Marlow is horrified by these "moribund shapes"—"phantoms"—dying of exhaustion and malnutrition "as in some picture of a massacre or a pestilence." Yet we wait in vain for Marlow to protest to anyone, though he soon encounters the chief accountant of the station, an impeccably dressed and groomed Englishman. There is the suggestion in "Heart of Darkness," as elsewhere in Conrad's work, of a pessimism so deeply entrenched as to be identical with a self-serving political conservatism that conveniently renders any form of activism, even protest, ineffective. For if all men harbor darkness in their hearts, why try to save them? Why even pity them?

The famous tale "The Secret Sharer," from Conrad's collection 'Twixt Land and Sea (1912), similarly reflects the narrowness of its creator's perspective. Here it is class, not sex or race, that determines a man's worth: an immature young captain, uneasy in his responsibility, mysteriously protects a fugitive named Leggatt, who has fled another ship after having killed a man; the young captain goes to extraordinary, foolhardy risks to allow Leggatt to escape being brought back to England to be tried; by the end of the suspense story, with the flight of Leggatt, the equation between the two men, forged out of their similar backgrounds and temperaments, has been many times reiterated: Leggatt swims clear of the ship "as though he were my second self . . . a free man, a proud swimmer striking out for a new destiny."

The difficulty for contemporary readers of "The Secret Sharer," which was one of Conrad's favorites among his own stories, is that the bond immediately forged between the young captain and the young fugitive is class-ordained and narcissistic: Leggatt has even attended the captain's school, Conway ("You're a Conway boy?"). Leggatt's act of violence is portrayed as a virtuous act by an upstanding if hot-headed first mate; the man he has killed is of a lower social rank, one of the common sailors: "He wouldn't do his duty and wouldn't let anybody else do theirs. . . . You know well the sort of ill-conditioned snarling cur—" Why does the young captain so eagerly take Leggatt at his own word, and make no attempt to verify the story?

> He appealed to me as if our experiences had been as identical as our clothes. And I knew well enough the pestiferous danger of such a character where there are no means of legal repression. And I knew well enough also that my double there was no homicidal ruffian. I did not think of asking him for details, and he told me the story roughly in brusque, disconnected sentences. I needed no more. I saw it all going on as though I were myself inside that other sleeping suit.

Where the Doppelgänger ("double") relationship between Marlow and Kurtz is mysterious, subtle and ever-shifting in its meanings, the relationship between the captain and Leggatt is superficial and far too heavily underscored. But "The Secret Sharer" remains one of Conrad's most characteristic stories, and it contains passages of language as beautifully evocative as the most celebrated passages in "Heart of Darkness." The opening is particularly effective, setting the tone for a tale of solitary risk and initiation:

> On my right hand there were lines of fishing stakes resembling a mysterious system of half-submerged bamboo fences, incomprehensible in its division of the domain of tropical fishes, and crazy of aspect as if abandoned forever by some nomad tribe . . . for there

was no sign of human habitation as far as the eye
could reach.

The silent approach of Leggatt, like a phantom in a
dream:

> The side of the ship made an opaque belt of shadow
> on the darkling glassy shimmer of the sea. But I saw
> at once something elongated and pale floating very
> close to the ladder. Before I could form a guess a faint
> flash of phosphorescent light, which seemed to issue
> suddenly from the naked body of a man, flickered in
> the sleeping water with the elusive, silent play of sum-
> mer lightning in a night sky. With a gasp I saw re-
> vealed to my stare a pair of feet, the long legs, a broad
> livid back immersed right up to the neck in a greenish
> cadaverous glow. One hand, awash, clutched the bot-
> tom rung of the ladder. He was complete except for
> the head. A headless corpse!

As if the young captain is the "head," the conscious-
ness; and the romantic fugitive Leggatt the "body,"
the physical being and "secret sharer."

If Conrad's ideal in writing is to make us *see*, "The
Secret Sharer," as brilliantly as "Heart of Darkness,"
frequently fulfills that ideal.

All enduring works of art—whether Homer's *Iliad*
and *Odyssey*, the tragedies of William Shakespeare,
the popular novels of Honoré de Balzac, Charles
Dickens, Mark Twain, as well as the more literary,
esoteric novels of Joseph Conrad, Virginia Woolf, and
James Joyce—bear the imprint of their time, place,
and social perspective. All art is selective and therefore, from some perspective, unfair; no art can be universal, for no artist is universal; we are all local
individuals, shaped by the customs of our tribes. The
enduring artist is the creator not of perfect works but
of works that transcend the circumstances of their creation and contribute to the aesthetic development of
their craft. One need not identify with a writer's cul-
tural perspective to recognize that he or she may be

possessed of unique, valuable gifts; like Joseph Conrad, an artist whose fiction repays close and repeated
readings and whose unsparing tragic vision has a particular resonance for the twentieth century with its
blood-tide of history—the devastation of two world
wars and countless nearly continuous smaller wars, the
unspeakable horror of the Holocaust, the slaughter of
hundreds of millions of men, women and children in
the service of deranged totalitarian "ideals." Joseph
Conrad is one of the great visionaries bearing witness
to the predicament of civilized man: how to match the
"technique" and "method" so ironically celebrated in
"Heart of Darkness" with a corresponding humanity
that acknowledges, but does not succumb to, man's
flawed and treacherous soul.

The Secret Sharer

I

On my right hand there were lines of fishing stakes resembling a mysterious system of half-submerged bamboo fences, incomprehensible in its division of the domain of tropical fishes, and crazy of aspect as if abandoned forever by some nomad tribe of fishermen now gone to the other end of the ocean; for there was no sign of human habitation as far as the eye could reach. To the left a group of barren islets, suggesting ruins of stone walls, towers, and blockhouses, had its foundations set in a blue sea that itself looked solid, so still and stable did it lie below my feet; even the track of light from the westering sun shone smoothly, without that animated glitter which tells of an imperceptible ripple. And when I turned my head to take a parting glance at the tug which had just left us anchored outside the bar, I saw the straight line of the flat shore joined to the stable sea, edge to edge, with a perfect and unmarked closeness, in one leveled floor half brown, half blue under the enormous dome of the sky. Corresponding in their insignificance to the islets of the sea, two small clumps of trees, one on each side of the only fault in the impeccable joint, marked the mouth of the river Meinam we had just left on the first preparatory stage of our homeward journey; and, far back on the inland level, a larger and loftier mass, the grove surrounding the great Paknam pagoda, was the only thing on which the eye could rest from the vain task of exploring the monotonous sweep of the horizon. Here and there gleams as of a few scattered pieces of silver marked the windings of the great river; and on the nearest of them, just within the bar, the tug steaming right into the land became lost to my sight, hull and funnel and masts, as though the impassive earth had swallowed her up without an effort, without a tremor. My eye followed the light cloud of her smoke, now here, now there, above the plain, according to the devious curves of the stream, but always fainter and farther away, till I lost it at last behind the miter-shaped hill of the great pagoda. And then I was left alone with my ship, anchored at the head of the Gulf of Siam.

She floated at the starting point of a long journey, very still in an immense stillness, the shadows of her spars flung far to the eastward by the setting sun. At that moment I was alone on her decks. There was not a sound in her—and around us nothing moved, nothing lived, not a canoe on the water, not a bird in the air, not a cloud in the sky. In this breathless pause at the threshold of a long passage we seemed to be measuring our fitness for a long and arduous enterprise, the appointed task of both our existences to be carried out, far from all human eyes, with only sky and sea for spectators and for judges.

There must have been some glare in the air to interfere with one's sight, because it was only just before the sun left us that my roaming eyes made out beyond the highest ridges of the principal islet of the group something which did away with the solemnity of perfect solitude. The tide of darkness flowed on swiftly; and with tropical suddenness a swarm of stars came out above the shadowy earth, while I lingered yet, my hand resting lightly on my ship's rail as if on the shoulder of a trusted friend. But, with all that multitude of celestial bodies staring down at one, the comfort of quiet communion with her was gone for good. And there were also disturbing sounds by this time—voices, footsteps, forward; the steward flitted along the maindeck, a busily ministering spirit; a hand bell tinkled urgently under the poop deck. . . .

I found my two officers waiting for me near the supper table, in the lighted cuddy. We sat down at once, and as I helped the chief mate, I said:

"Are you aware that there is a ship anchored inside the islands? I saw her mastheads above the ridge as the sun went down."

He raised sharply his simple face, overcharged by a terrible growth of whisker, and emitted his usual ejaculations: "Bless my soul, sir! You don't say so!"

My second mate was a round-cheeked, silent young man, grave beyond his years, I thought; but as our eyes happened to meet I detected a slight quiver on his lips. I looked down at once. It was not my part to encourage sneering on board my ship. It must be said, too, that I knew very little of my officers. In consequence of certain events of no particular significance, except to myself, I had been appointed to the command only a fortnight before. Neither did I know much of the hands forward. All these people had been together for eighteen months or so, and my position was that of the only stranger on board. I mention this because it has some bearing on what is to follow. But what I felt most was my being a stranger to the ship; and if all the truth must be told, I was somewhat of a stranger to myself. The youngest man on board (barring the second mate), and untried as yet by a position of the fullest responsibility, I was willing to take the adequacy of the others for granted. They had simply to be equal to their tasks; but I wondered how far I should turn out faithful to that ideal conception of one's own personality every man sets up for himself secretly.

Meantime the chief mate, with an almost visible effect of collaboration on the past of his round eyes and frightful whiskers, was trying to evolve a theory of the anchored ship. His dominant trait was to take all things into earnest consideration. He was of a painstaking turn of mind. As he used to say, he "liked to account to himself" for practically everything that came in his way, down to a miserable scorpion he had found in his cabin a week before. The why and the wherefore of that scorpion—how it got on board and came to select his room rather than the pantry (which was a dark place and more what a scorpion would be partial to), and how on earth it managed to drown itself in the inkwell of his writing desk—had exercised him infinitely. The ship within the islands was much more easily accounted for; and just as we were about to rise from table he made his pronouncement. She was, he doubted not, a ship from home lately arrived. Probably she drew too much water to cross the bar except at the top of spring tides. Therefore she went into that natural harbor to wait for a few days in preference to remaining in an open roadstead.

"That's so," confirmed the second mate, suddenly, in his slightly hoarse voice. "She draws over twenty feet. She's the Liverpool ship *Sephora* with a cargo of coal. Hundred and twenty-three days from Cardiff."

We looked at him in surprise.

"The tugboat skipper told me when he came on board for your letters, sir," explained the young man. "He expects to take her up the river the day after tomorrow."

After thus overwhelming us with the extent of his information he slipped out of the cabin. The mate observed regretfully that he "could not account for that young fellow's whims." What prevented him telling us all about it at once, he wanted to know.

I detained him as he was making a move. For the last two days the crew had had plenty of hard work, and the night before they had very little sleep. I felt painfully that I—a stranger—was doing something unusual when I directed him to let all hands turn in without setting an anchor watch. I proposed to keep on deck myself till one o'clock or thereabouts. I would get the second mate to relieve me at that hour.

"He will turn out the cook and the steward at four," I concluded, "and then give you a call. Of course at the slightest sign of any sort of wind we'll have the hands up and make a start at once."

He concealed his astonishment. "Very well, sir." Outside the cuddy he put his head in the second mate's door to inform him of my unheard-of caprice to take a five hours' anchor watch on myself. I heard the other raise his voice incredulously—"What? The Captain himself?" Then a few more murmurs, a door closed, then another. A few moments later I went on deck.

My strangeness, which had made me sleepless, had prompted that unconventional arrangement, as if I had expected in those solitary hours of the night to get on terms with the ship of which I knew nothing, manned by men of whom I knew very little more. Fast alongside a wharf, littered like any ship in port with a tangle of unrelated things, invaded by unrelated shore people, I had hardly seen her yet properly. Now, as she lay cleared for sea, the stretch of her main-deck seemed to me very fine under the stars. Very fine, very roomy for her size, and very inviting. I descended the poop and paced the waist, my mind picturing to myself the coming passage through the Malay Archipelago, down the Indian Ocean, and up the Atlantic. All its phases were familiar enough to me, every characteristic, all the alternatives which were likely to face me on the high seas—everything! . . . except the novel responsibility of command. But I took heart from the reasonable thought that the ship was like other ships, the men like other men, and that the sea was not likely to keep any special surprises expressly for my discomfiture.

Arrived at that comforting conclusion, I bethought myself of a cigar and went below to get it. All was still down there. Everybody at the after end of the ship was sleeping profoundly. I came out again on the quarter-deck, agreeably at ease in my sleeping suit on that warm breathless night, barefooted, a glowing cigar in my teeth, and, going forward, I was met by the profound silence of the fore end of the ship. Only as I passed the door of the forecastle I heard a deep, quite, trustful sigh of some sleeper inside. And suddenly I rejoiced in the great security of the sea as compared with the unrest of the land, in my choice of that untempted life presenting no disquieting problems, invested with an elementary moral beauty by the

absolute straightforwardness of its appeal and by the
singleness of its purpose.

The riding light in the forerigging burned with a
clear, untroubled, as if symbolic, flame, confident and
bright in the mysterious shades of the night. Passing
on my way aft along the other side of the ship, I
observed that the rope side ladder, put over, no doubt,
for the master of the tug when he came to fetch away
our letters, had not been hauled in as it should have
been. I became annoyed at this, for exactitude in some
small matters is the very soul of discipline. Then I
reflected that I had myself peremptorily dismissed my
officers from duty, and by my own act had prevented
the anchor watch being formally set and things properly attended to. I asked myself whether it was wise
ever to interfere with the established routine of duties
even from the kindest of motives. My action might
have made me appear eccentric. Goodness only knew
how that absurdly whiskered mate would "account"
for my conduct, and what the whole ship thought of
that informality of their new captain. I was vexed
with myself.

Not from compunction certainly, but, as it were me-
chanically, I proceeded to get the ladder in myself.
Now a side ladder of that sort is a light affair and
comes in easily, yet my vigorous tug, which should
have brought it flying on board, merely recoiled upon
my body in a totally unexpected jerk. What the
devil! . . . I was so astounded by the immovableness
of that ladder that I remained stockstill, trying to account for it to myself like that imbecile mate of mine.
In the end, of course, I put my head over the rail.

The side of the ship made an opaque belt of shadow
on the darkling glassy shimmer of the sea. But I saw
at once something elongated and pale floating very
close to the ladder. Before I could form a guess a faint
flash of phosphorescent light, which seemed to issue
suddenly from the naked body of a man, flickered in
the sleeping water with the elusive, silent play of sum-
mer lightning in a night sky. With a gasp I saw re-
vealed to my stare a pair of feet, the long legs, a broad

livid back immersed right up to the neck in a greenish cadaverous glow. One hand, awash, clutched the bottom rung of the ladder. He was complete but for the head. A headless corpse! The cigar dropped out of my gaping mouth with a tiny plop and a short hiss quite audible in the absolute stillness of all things under heaven. At that I suppose he raised up his face, a dimly pale oval in the shadow of the ship's side. But even then I could only barely make out down there the shape of his black-haired head. However, it was enough for the horrid, frost-bound sensation which had gripped me about the chest to pass off. The moment of vain exclamations was past, too. I only climbed on the spare spar and leaned over the rail as far as I could, to bring my eyes nearer to that mystery floating alongside.

As he hung by the ladder, like a resting swimmer, the sea lightning played about his limbs at every stir; and he appeared in it ghastly, silvery, fishlike. He remained as mute as a fish, too. He made no motion to get out of the water, either. It was inconceivable that he should not attempt to come on board, and strangely troubling to suspect that perhaps he did not want to. And my first words were prompted by just that troubled incertitude.

"What's the matter?" I asked in my ordinary tone, speaking down to the face upturned exactly under mine.

"Cramp," it answered, no louder. Then slightly anxious, 'I say, no need to call anyone."

"I was not going to," I said.

"Are you alone on deck?"

"Yes."

I had somehow the impression that he was on the point of letting go the ladder to swim away beyond my ken—mysterious as he came. But, for the moment, this being appearing as he had risen from the bottom of the sea (it was certainly the nearest land to the ship) wanted only to know the time. I told him. And he, down there, tentatively:

"I suppose your captain's turned in?"

"I am sure he isn't," I said.

He seemed to struggle with himself, for I heard something like the low, bitter murmur of doubt. "What's the good?" His next words came out with a hesitating effort.

"Look here, my man. Could you call him out quietly?"

I thought the time had come to declare myself.

"*I* am the captain."

I heard a "By Jove!' whispered at the level of the water. The phosphorescence flashed in the swirl of the water all about his limbs, his other hand seized the ladder.

"My name's Leggatt."

The voice was calm and resolute. A good voice. The self-possession of that man had somehow induced a corresponding state in myself. It was very quietly that I remarked:

"You must be a good swimmer."

"Yes. I've been in the water practically since nine o'clock. The question for me now is whether I am to let go this ladder and go on swimming till I sink from exhaustion, or—to come on board here."

I felt this was no mere formula of desperate speech, but a real alternative in the view of a strong soul. I should have gathered from this that he was young; indeed, it is only the young who are ever confronted by such clear issues. But at the time it was pure intuition on my part. A mysterious communication was established already between us two—in the face of that silent, darkened tropical sea. I was young, too; young enough to make no comment. The man in the water began suddenly to climb up the ladder, and I hastened away from the rail to fetch some clothes.

Before entering the cabin I stood still, listening in the lobby at the foot of the stairs. A faint snore came through the closed door of the chief mate's room. The second mate's door was on the hook, but the darkness in there was absolutely soundless. He, too, was young and could sleep like a stone. Remained the steward, but he was not likely to wake up before he was called.

I got a sleeping suit out of my room and, coming back
on deck, saw the naked man from the sea sitting on
the main hatch, glimmering white in the darkness, his
elbows on his knees and his head in his hands. In a
moment he had concealed his damp body in a sleeping
suit of the same gray-stripe pattern as the one I was
wearing and followed me like my double on the poop.
Together we moved right aft, barefooted, silent.

"What is it?" I asked in a deadened voice, taking
the lighted lamp out of the binnacle, and raising it to
his face.

"An ugly business."

He had rather regular features; a good mouth; light
eyes under somewhat heavy, dark eyebrows; a smooth,
square forehead; no growth on his cheeks; a small,
brown mustache, and a well-shaped, round chin. His
expression was concentrated, meditative, under the in-
specting light of the lamp I held up to his face; such
as a man thinking hard in solitude might wear. My
sleeping suit was just right for his size. A well-knit
young fellow of twenty-five at most. He caught his
lower lip with the edge of white, even teeth.

"Yes," I said, replacing the lamp in the binnacle.
The warm, heavy tropical night closed upon his head
again.

"There's a ship over there," he murmured.

"Yes, I know. The *Sephora*. Did you know of us?"

"Hadn't the slightest idea. I am the mate of her——"
He paused and corrected himself. "I should say I
was."

"Aha! Something wrong?"

"Yes. Very wrong indeed. I've killed a man."

"What do you mean? Just now?"

"No, on the passage. Weeks ago. Thirty-nine south.
When I say a man——"

"Fit of temper," I suggested, confidently.

The shadowy, dark head, like mine, seemed to nod
imperceptibly above the ghostly gray of my sleeping
suit. It was, in the night, as though I had been faced
by my own reflection in the depths of a somber and
immense mirror.

"A pretty thing to have to own up to for a Conway boy," murmured my double, distinctly.

"You're a Conway boy?"

"I am," he said, as if startled. Then, slowly . . . "Perhaps you too——"

It was so; but being a couple of years older I had left before he joined. After a quick interchange of dates a silence fell; and I thought suddenly of my absurd mate with his terrific whiskers and the "Bless my soul—you don't say so" type of intellect. My double gave me an inkling of his thoughts by saying: "My father's a parson in Norfolk. Do you see me before a judge and jury on that charge? For myself I can't see the necessity. There are fellows that an angel from heaven—— And I am not that. He was one of those creatures that are just simmering all the time with a silly sort of wickedness. Miserable devils that have no business to live at all. He wouldn't do his duty and wouldn't let anybody else do theirs. But what's the good of talking! You know well enough the sort of ill-conditioned snarling cur——"

He appealed to me as if our experiences had been as identical as our clothes. And I knew well enough the pestiferous danger of such a character where there are no means of legal repression. And I knew well enough also that my double there was no homicidal ruffian. I did not think of asking him for details, and he told me the story roughly in brusque, disconnected sentences. I needed no more. I saw it all going on as though I were myself inside that other sleeping suit.

"It happened while we were setting a reefed foresail, at dusk. Reefed foresail! You understand the sort of weather. The only sail we had left to keep the ship running; so you may guess what it had been like for days. Anxious sort of job, that. He gave me some of his cursed insolence at the sheet. I tell you I was overdone with this terrific weather that seemed to have no end to it. Terrific, I tell you—and a deep ship. I believe the fellow himself was half crazed with funk. It was no time for gentlemanly reproof, so I turned round and felled him like an ox. He up and at me.

We closed just as an awful sea made for the ship. All hands saw it coming and took to the rigging, but I had him by the throat, and went on shaking him like a rat, the men above us yelling, 'Look out! look out!' Then a crash as if the sky had fallen on my head. They say that for over ten minutes hardly anything was to be seen of the ship—just the three masts and a bit of the forecastle head and of the poop all awash driving along in a smother of foam. It was a miracle that they found us, jammed together behind the forebitts. It's clear that I meant business, because I was holding him by the throat still when they picked us up. He was black in the face. It was too much for them. It seems they rushed us aft together, gripped as we were, screaming 'Murder!' like a lot of lunatics, and broke into the cuddy. And the ship running for her life, touch and go all the time, any minute her last in a sea fit to turn your hair gray only a-looking at it. I understand that the skipper, too, started raving like the rest of them. The man had been deprived of sleep for more than a week, and to have this sprung on him at the height of a furious gale nearly drove him out of his mind. I wonder they didn't fling me overboard after getting the carcass of their precious shipmate out of my fingers. They had rather a job to separate us, I've been told. A sufficiently fierce story to make an old judge and a respectable jury sit up a bit. The first thing I heard when I came to myself was the maddening howling of that endless gale, and on that the voice of the old man. He was hanging on to my bunk, staring into my face out of the sou'wester.

" 'Mr. Leggatt, you have killed a man. You can act no longer as chief mate of this ship.' "

His care to subdue his voice made it sound monotonous. He rested a hand on the end of the skylight to steady himself with, and all that time did not stir a limb, so far as I could see. "Nice little tale for a quiet tea party," he concluded in the same tone.

One of my hands, too, rested on the end of the skylight; neither did I stir a limb, so far as I knew. We stood less than a foot from each other. It occurred

to me that if old "Bless my soul—you don't say so"
were to put his head up the companion and catch sight
to us, he would think he was seeing double, or imagine
himself come upon a scene of weird witchcraft; the
strange captain having a quiet confabulation by the
wheel with his own gray ghost. I became very much
concerned to prevent anything of the sort. I heard the
other's soothing undertone.

"My father's a parson in Norfolk," it said. Evidently
he had forgotten he had told me this important fact
before. Truly a nice little tale.

"You had better slip down into my stateroom now,"
I said, moving off stealthily. My double followed my
movements; our bare feet made no sound; I let him
in, closed the door with care, and, after giving a call
to the second mate, returned on deck for my relief.

"Not much sign of any wind yet," I remarked when
he approached.

"No, sir. Not much," he assented, sleepily, in his
hoarse voice, with just enough deference, no more,
and barely suppressing a yawn.

"Well, that's all you have a look out for. You have
got your orders."

"Yes, sir."

I paced a turn or two on the poop and saw him
take up his position face forward with his elbow in
the ratlines of the mizzen rigging before I went below.
The mate's faint snoring was still going on peacefully.
The cuddy lamp was burning over the table on which
stood a vase with flowers, a polite attention from the
ship's provision merchant—the last flowers we should
see for the next three months at the very least. Two
bunches of bananas hung from the beam symmetri-
cally, one on each side of the rudder casing. Everything was as before in the ship—except that two of
her captain's sleeping suits were simultaneously in use,
one motionless in the cuddy, the other keeping very
still in the captain's stateroom.

It must be explained here that my cabin had the
form of the capital letter L, the door being within the
angle and opening into the short part of the letter. A

couch was to the left, the bed place to the right; my writing desk and the chronometers' table faced the door. But anyone opening it, unless he stepped right inside, had no view of what I call the long (or vertical) part of the letter. It contained some lockers surmounted by a bookcase; and a few clothes, a thick jacket or two, caps, oilskin coat, and such like, hung on hooks. There was at the bottom of that part of a door opening into my bathroom, which could be entered also directly from the saloon. But that way was never used.

The mysterious arrival had discovered the advantage of this particular shape. Entering my room, lighted strongly by a big bulkhead lamp swung on gimbals above my writing desk, I did not see him anywhere till he stepped out quietly from behind the coats hung in the recessed part.

"I heard somebody moving about, and went in there at once," he whispered.

I, too, spoke under my breath.

"Nobody is likely to come in here without knocking and getting permission."

He nodded. His face was thin and the sunburn faded, as though he had been ill. And no wonder. He had been, I heard presently, kept under arrest in his cabin for nearly seven weeks. But there was nothing sickly in his eyes or in his expression. He was not a bit like me, really; yet, as we stood leaning over my bed place, whispering side by side, with our dark heads together and our backs to the door, anybody bold enough to open it stealthily would have been treated to the uncanny sight of a double captain busy talking in whispers with his other self.

"But all this doesn't tell me how you came to hang on to our side ladder," I inquired, in the hardly audible murmurs we used, after he had told me something more of the proceedings on board the *Sephora* once the bad weather was over.

"When we sighted Java Head I had had time to think all those matters out several times over. I had six weeks of doing nothing else, and with only an hour or so every evening for a tramp on the quarter-deck."

He whispered, his arms folded on the side of my bed place, staring through the open port. And I could imagine perfectly the manner of this thinking out—a stubborn if not a steadfast operation; something of which I should have been perfectly incapable.

"I reckoned it would be dark before we closed with the land," he continued, so low that I had to strain my hearing near as we were to each other, shoulder touching shoulder almost. "So I asked to speak to the old man. He always seemed very sick when he came to see me—as if he could not look me in the face. You know, that foresail saved the ship. She was too deep to have run long under bare poles. And it was I that managed to set it for him. Anyway, he came. When I had him in my cabin—he stood by the door looking at me as if I had the halter round my neck already—I asked him right away to leave my cabin door unlocked at night while the ship was going through Sunda Straits. There would be the Java coast within two or three miles, off Angier Point. I wanted nothing more. I've had a prize for swimming my second year in the Conway."

"I can believe it," I breathed out.

"God only knows why they locked me in every night. To see some of their faces you'd have thought they were afraid I'd go about at night strangling people. Am I a murdering brute? Do I look it? By Jove! If I had been he wouldn't have trusted himself like that into my room. You'll say I might have chucked him aside and bolted out, there and then—it was dark already. Well, no. And for the same reason I wouldn't think of trying to smash the door. There would have been a rush to stop me at the noise, and I did not mean to get into a confounded scrimmage. Somebody else might have got killed—for I would not have broken out only to get chucked back, and I did not want any more of that work. He refused, looking more sick than ever. He was afraid of the men, and also of that old second mate of his who had been sailing with him for years—a gray-headed old humbug; and his steward, too, had been with him devil knows how long—seventeen years or more—a dogmatic sort of loafer who hated me like poison, just because I was the chief mate. No chief mate ever made more than one voyage in the *Sephora*, you know. Those two old chaps ran the ship. Devil only knows what the skipper wasn't afraid of (all his nerve went to pieces altogether in that hellish spell of bad weather we had)—of what the law would do to him—of his wife, perhaps. Oh, yes! she's on board. Though I don't think she would have meddled. She would have been only too glad to have me out of the ship in any way. The 'brand of Cain' business, don't you see. That's all right. I was ready enough to go off wandering on the face of the earth—and that was price enough to pay for an Abel of that sort. Anyhow, he wouldn't listen to me. 'This thing must take its course. I represent the law here.' He was shaking like a leaf. 'So you won't?' 'No!' 'Then I hope you will be able to sleep on that,' I said, and turned my back on him. 'I wonder that *you* can,' cries he, and locks the door.

"Well after that, I couldn't. Not very well. That was three weeks ago. We have had a slow passage through the Java Sea; drifted about Carimata for ten days. When we anchored here they thought, I suppose, it was all right. The nearest land (and that's five miles) is the ship's destination; the consul would soon set about catching me; and there would have been no object in bolting to these islets there. I don't suppose there's a drop of water on them. I don't know how it was, but tonight that steward, after bringing me my supper, went out to let me eat it, and left the door unlocked. And I ate it—all there was, too. After I had finished I strolled out on the quarter-deck. I don't know that I meant to do anything. A breath of fresh air was all I wanted, I believe. Then a sudden temptation came over me. I kicked off my slippers and was in the water before I had made up my mind fairly. Somebody heard the splash and they raised an awful hullabaloo. 'He's gone! Lower the boats! He's com-

mitted suicide! No, he's swimming.' Certainly I was
swimming. It's not so easy for a swimmer like me to
commit suicide by drowning. I landed on the nearest
islet before the boat left the ship's side. I heard them
pulling about in the dark, hailing, and so on, but after
a bit they gave up. Everything quieted down and the
anchorage became as still as death. I sat down on a
stone and began to think. I felt certain they would
start searching for me at daylight. There was no place
to hide on those stony things—and if there had been,
what would have been the good? But now I was clear
of that ship, I was not going back. So after a while I
took off all my clothes, tied them up in a bundle with
a stone inside, and dropped them in the deep water
on the outer side of that islet. That was suicide enough
for me. Let them think what they liked, but I didn't
mean to drown myself. I meant to swim till I sank—
but that's not the same thing. I struck out for another
of these little islands, and it was from that one that I
first saw your riding light. Something to swim for. I
went on easily, and on the way I came upon a flat
rock or two above water. In the daytime, I dare say,
you might make it out with a glass from your poop. I
scrambled up on it and rested myself for a bit. Then
I made another start. That last spell must have been
over a mile."

His whisper was getting fainter and fainter, and all
the time he stared straight out through the porthole,
in which there was not even a star to be seen. I had
not interrupted him. There was something that made
comment impossible in his narrative, or perhaps in
himself; a sort of feeling, a quality, which I can't find
a name for. And when he ceased, all I found was a
futile whisper: "So you swam for our light?"

"Yes—straight for it. It was something to swim for.
I couldn't see any stars low down because the coast
was in the way, and I couldn't see the land, either.
The water was like glass. One might have been swimming in a confounded thousand-feet deep cistern with
no place for scrambling out anywhere; but what I
didn't like was the notion of swimming round and

round like a crazed bullock before I gave out; and as I didn't mean to go back . . . No. Do you see me being hauled back, stark naked, off one of these little islands by the scruff of the neck and fighting like a wild beast? Somebody would have got killed for certain, and I did not want any of that. So I went on. Then your ladder——"

"Why didn't you hail the ship?" I asked, a little louder.

He touched my shoulder lightly. Lazy footsteps came right over our heads and stopped. The second mate had crossed from the other side of the poop and might have been hanging over the rail for all we knew.

"He couldn't hear us talking—could he?" My double breathed into my very ear, anxiously.

His anxiety was in answer, a sufficient answer, to the question I had put to him. An answer containing all the difficulty of that situation. I closed the porthole quietly, to make sure. A louder word might have been overheard.

"Who's that?" he whispered then.

"My second mate. But I don't know much more of the fellow than you do."

And I told him a little about myself. I had been appointed to take charge while I least expected anything of the sort, not quite a fortnight ago. I didn't know either the ship or the people. Hadn't had the time in port to look about me or size anybody up. And as to the crew, all they knew was that I was appointed to take the ship home. For the rest, I was almost as much of a stranger on board as himself, I said. And at the moment I felt it most acutely. I felt that it would take very little to make me a suspect person in the eyes of the ship's company.

He had turned about meantime; and we, the two strangers in the ship, faced each other in identical attitudes.

"Your ladder——" he murmured, after a silence. "Who'd have thought of finding a ladder hanging over at night in a ship anchored out here! I felt just then a very unpleasant faintness. After the life I've been

leading for nine weeks, anybody would have got out
of condition. I wasn't capable of swimming round as
far as your rudder chains. And, lo and behold! there
was a ladder to get hold of. After I gripped it I said
to myself, 'What's the good?'' When I saw a man's
head looking over I thought I would swim away presently and leave him shouting—in whatever language
it was. I didn't mind being looked at. I—I liked it.
And then you speaking to me so quietly—as if you
had expected me—made me hold on a little longer. It
had been a confounded lonely time—I don't mean
while swimming. I was glad to talk a little to somebody
that didn't belong to the *Sephora*. As to asking for
the captain, that was a mere impulse. It could have
been no use, with all the ship knowing about me and
the other people pretty certain to be round here in
the morning. I don't know—I wanted to be seen, to
talk with somebody, before I went on. I don't know
what I would have said. . . . 'Fine night, isn't it?' or
something of the sort.''

"Do you think they will be round here presently?''
I asked with some incredulity.

"Quite likely,'' he said, faintly.

He looked extremely haggard all of a sudden. His
head rolled on his shoulders.

"H'm. We shall see then. Meantime get into that
bed,'' I whispered. "Want help? There.''

It was a rather high bed place with a set of drawers
underneath. This amazing swimmer really needed the
lift I gave him by seizing his leg. He tumbled in, rolled
over on his back, and flung one arm across his eyes.
And then, with his face nearly hidden, he must have
looked exactly as I used to look in that bed. I gazed
upon my other self for a while before drawing across
carefully the two green serge curtains which ran on a
brass rod. I thought for a moment of pinning them
together for greater safety, but I sat down on the
couch, and once there I felt unwilling to rise and hunt
for a pin. I would do it in a moment. I was extremely
tired, in a peculiarly intimate way, by the strain of
stealthiness, by the effort of whispering and the gen-

eral secrecy of this excitement. It was three o'clock by
now and I had been on my feet since nine, but I was
not sleepy; I could not have gone to sleep. I sat there,
fagged out, looking at the curtains, trying to clear my
mind of the confused sensation of being in two places
at once, and greatly bothered by an exasperating
knocking in my head. It was a relief to discover suddenly that it was not in my head at all, but on the
outside of the door. Before I could collect myself the
words "Come in" were out of my mouth, and the
steward entered with a tray, bringing in my morning
coffee. I had slept, after all, and I was so frightened
that I shouted, "This way! I am here, steward," as
though he had been miles away. He put down the tray
on the table next the couch and only then said, very
quietly, "I can see you are here, sir." I felt him give
me a keen look, but I dared not meet his eyes just
then. He must have wondered why I had drawn the
curtains of my bed before going to sleep on the couch.
He went out, hooking the door open as usual.

I heard the crew washing decks above me. I knew
I would have been told at once if there had been any
wind. Calm, I thought, and I was doubly vexed. Indeed, I felt dual more than ever. The steward reap-
peared suddenly in the doorway. I jumped up from
the couch so quickly that he gave a start.

"What do you want here?"

"Close your port, sir—they are washing decks."

"It is closed," I said, reddening.

"Very well, sir." But he did not move from the
doorway and returned my stare in an extraordinary,
equivocal manner for a time. Then his eyes wavered,
all his expression changed, and in a voice unusually
gentle, almost coaxingly:

"May I come in to take the empty cup away, sir?"

"Of course!" I turned my back on him while he
popped in and out. Then I unhooked and closed the
door and even pushed the bolt. This sort of thing
could not go on very long. The cabin was as hot as
an oven, too. I took a peep at my double, and discovered that he had not moved, his arm was still over his

eyes; but his chest heaved; his hair was wet; his chin
glistened with perspiration. I reached over him and
opened the port.

"I must show myself on deck," I reflected.

Of course, theoretically, I could do what I liked,
with no one to say nay to me within the whole circle
of the horizon; but to lock my cabin door and take
the key away I did not dare. Directly I put my head
out of the companion I saw the group of my two officers, the second mate barefooted, the chief mate in
long India-rubber boots, near the break of the poop,
and the steward halfway down the poop ladder talking
to them eagerly. He happened to catch sight of me
and dived, the second ran down on the main-deck
shouting some order or other, and the chief mate came
to meet me, touching his cap.

There was a sort of curiosity in his eye that I did
not like. I don't know whether the steward had told
them that I was "queer" only, or downright drunk,
but I know the man meant to have a good look at
me. I watched him coming with a smile which, as he
got into point-blank range, took effect and froze his
very whiskers. I did not give him time to open his lips.

"Square the yards by lifts and braces before the
hands go to breakfast."

It was the first particular order I had given on board
that ship; and I stayed on deck to see it executed, too.
I had felt the need of asserting myself without loss of
time. That sneering young cub got taken down a peg
or two on that occasion, and I also seized the opportunity of having a good look at the face of every fore-
mast man as they filed past me to go to the after
braces. At breakfast time, eating nothing myself, I pre-
sided with such frigid dignity that the two mates were
only too glad to escape from the cabin as soon as
decency permitted; and all the time the dual working
of my mind distracted me almost to the point of insanity. I was constantly watching myself, my secret self,
as dependent on my actions as my own personality,
sleeping in that bed, behind that door which faced me
as I sat at the head of the table. It was very much like

being mad, only it was worse because one was aware of it.

I had to shake him for a solid minute, but when at last he opened his eyes it was in the full possession of his senses, with an inquiring look.

"All's well so far," I whispered. "Now you must vanish into the bathroom."

He did so, as noiseless as a ghost, and then I rang for the steward, and facing him boldly, directed him to tidy up my stateroom while I was having my bath— "and be quick about it." As my tone admitted of no excuses, he said, "Yes, sir," and ran off to fetch his dustpan and brushes. I took a bath and did most of my dressing, splashing, and whistling softly for the steward's edification, while the secret sharer of my life stood drawn up bolt upright in that little space, his face looking very sunken in daylight, his eyelids lowered under the stern, dark line of his eyebrows drawn together by a slight frown.

When I left him there to go back to my room the steward was finishing dusting. I sent for the mate and engaged him in some insignificant conversation. It was, as it were, trifling with the terrific character of his whiskers; but my object was to give him an opportunity for a good look at my cabin. And then I could at last shut, with a clear conscience, the door of my stateroom and get my double back into the recessed part. There was nothing else for it. He had to sit still on a small folding stool, half smothered by the heavy coats hanging there. We listened to the steward going into the bathroom out of the saloon, filling the water bottles there, scrubbing the bath, settling things to rights, whisk, bang, clatter—out again into the saloon—turn the key—click. Such was my scheme for keeping my second self invisible. Nothing better could be contrived under the circumstances. And there we sat; I at my writing desk ready to appear busy with some papers, he behind me out of sight of the door. It would not have been prudent to talk in daytime; and I could not have stood the excitement of that queer sense of whispering to myself. Now and then, glancing over my shoulder, I saw him far back there, sitting rigidly on the low stool, his bare feet close together, his arms folded, his head hanging on his breast—and perfectly still. Anybody would have taken him for me.

I was fascinated by it myself. Every moment I had to glance over my shoulder. I was looking at him when a voice outside the door said:

"Beg pardon, sir."

"Well!" . . . I kept my eyes on him, and so when the voice outside the door announced, "There's a ship's boat coming our way, sir," I saw him give a start—the first movement he had made for hours. But he did not raise his bowed head.

"All right. Get the ladder over."

I hesitated. Should I whisper something to him? But what? His immobility seemed to have been never disturbed. What could I tell him he did not know already? . . . Finally I went on deck.

II

The skipper of the *Sephora* had a thin red whisker all round his face, and the sort of complexion that goes with hair of that color; also the particular, rather smeary shade of blue in the eyes. He was not exactly a showy figure; his shoulders were high, his stature but middling—one leg slightly more bandy than the other. He shook hands, looking vaguely around. A spiritless tenacity was his main characteristic, I judged. I behaved with a politeness which seemed to disconcert him. Perhaps he was shy. He mumbled to me as if he were ashamed of what he was saying; gave his name (it was something like Archbold—but at this distance of years I hardly am sure), his ship's name, and a few other particulars of that sort, in the manner of a criminal making a reluctant and doleful confession. He had had terrible weather on the passage out—terrible—terrible—wife aboard, too.

By this time we were seated in the cabin and the steward brought in a tray with a bottle and glasses.

"Thanks! No." Never took liquor. Would have some water, though. He drank two tumblerfuls. Terrible thirsty work. Ever since daylight had been exploring the islands round his ship.

"What was that for—fun?" I asked, with an appearance of polite interest.

"No!" He sighed. "Painful duty."

As he persisted in his mumbling and I wanted my double to hear every word, I hit upon the notion of informing him that I regretted to say I was hard of hearing.

"Such a young man, too!" he nodded, keeping his smeary blue, unintelligent eyes fastened upon me. "What was the cause of it—some disease?" he inquired, without the least sympathy and as if he thought that, if so, I'd got no more than I deserved.

"Yes; disease," I admitted in a cheerful tone which seemed to shock him. But my point was gained, because he had to raise his voice to give me his tale. It is not worth while to record that version. It was just over two months since all this had happened, and he had thought so much about it that he seemed completely muddled as to its bearings, but still immensely impressed.

"What would you think of such a thing happening on board your own ship? I've had the *Sephora* for these fifteen years. I am a well-known shipmaster."

He was densely distressed—and perhaps I should have sympathized with him if I had been able to detach my mental vision from the unsuspected sharer of my cabin as though he were my second self. There he was on the other side of the bulkhead, four or five feet from us, no more, as we sat in the saloon. I looked politely at Captain Archbold (if that was his name), but it was the other I saw, in a gray sleeping suit, seated on a low stool, his bare feet close together, his arms folded, and every word said between us falling into the ears of his dark head bowed on his chest.

"I have been at sea now, man and boy, for seven-and-thirty years, and I've never heard of such a thing happening in an English ship. And that it should be my ship. Wife on board, too."

I was hardly listening to him.

"Don't you think," I said, "that the heavy sea which, you told me, came aboard just then might have killed the man? I have seen the sheer weight of a sea kill a man very neatly, by simply breaking his neck."

"Good God!" he uttered, impressively, fixing his smeary blue eyes on me. "The sea! No man killed by the sea ever looked like that." He seemed positively scandalized at my suggestion. And as I gazed at him certainly not prepared for anything original on his part, he advanced his head close to me and thrust his tongue out at me so suddenly that I couldn't help starting back.

After scoring over my calmness in this graphic way he nodded wisely. If I had seen the sight, he assured me, I would never forget it as long as I lived. The weather was too bad to give the corpse a proper sea burial. So next day at dawn they took it up on the poop, covering its face with a bit of bunting; he read a short prayer, and then, just as it was, in its oilskins and long boots, they launched it amongst those mountainous seas that seemed ready every moment to swallow up the ship herself and the terrified lives on board of her.

"That reefed foresail saved you," I threw in.

"Under God—it did," he exclaimed fervently. "It was by a special mercy, I firmly believe, that it stood some of those hurricane squalls."

"It was the setting of that sail which——" I began.

"God's own hand in it," he interrupted me. "Nothing less could have done it. I don't mind telling you that I hardly dared give the order. It seemed impossible that we could touch anything without losing it, and then our last hope would have been gone."

The terror of that gale was on him yet. I let him go on for a bit, then said, casually—as if returning to a minor subject:

"You were very anxious to give up your mate to the shore people, I believe?"

He was. To the law. His obscure tenacity on that point had in it something incomprehensible and a little awful; something, as it were, mystical, quite apart from his anxiety that he should not be suspected of "countenancing any doings of that sort." Seven-and-thirty virtuous years at sea, of which over twenty of immaculate command, and the last fifteen in the *Sephora,* seemed to have laid him under some pitiless obligation.

"And you know," he went on, groping shame-facedly amongst his feelings, "I did not engage that young fellow. His people had some interest with my owners. I was in a way forced to take him on. He looked very smart, very gentlemanly, and all that. But do you know—I never liked him, somehow. I am a plain man. You see, he wasn't exactly the sort for the chief mate of a ship like the *Sephora.*"

I had become so connected in thoughts and impressions with the secret sharer of my cabin that I felt as if I, personally, were being given to understand that I, too, was not the sort that would have done for the chief mate of a ship like the *Sephora.* I had no doubt of it in my mind.

"Not at all the style of man. You understand," he insisted, superfluously, looking hard at me.

I smiled urbanely. He seemed at a loss for a while.

"I suppose I must report a suicide."

"Beg pardon?"

"Sui-cide! That's what I'll have to write to my owners directly I get in."

"Unless you manage to recover him before tomorrow," I assented, dispassionately. . . . "I mean, alive."

He mumbled something which I really did not catch, and I turned my ear to him in a puzzled manner. He fairly bawled:

"The land—I say, the mainland is at least seven miles off my anchorage."

"About that."

My lack of excitement, of curiosity, of surprise, of any sort of pronounced interest, began to arouse his distrust. But except for the felicitous pretense of deafness I had not tried to pretend anything. I had felt utterly incapable of playing the part of ignorance

properly, and therefore was afraid to try. It is also
certain that he had brought some ready-made suspi-
cions with him, and that he viewed my politeness as
a strange and unnatural phenomenon. And yet how
else could I have received him? Not heartily! That was
impossible for psychological reasons, which I need not
state here. My only object was to keep off his inquiries. Surlily? Yes, but surliness might have provoked a
point-blank question. From its novelty to him and
from its nature, punctilious courtesy was the manner
best calculated to restrain the man. But there was the
danger of his breaking through my defense bluntly. I
could not, I think, have met him by a direct lie, also
for psychological (not moral) reasons. If he had only
known how afraid I was of his putting my feeling of
identity with the other to the test! But, strangely
enough—(I thought of it only afterwards)—I believe
that he was not a little disconcerted by the reverse
side of that weird situation, by something in me that
reminded him of the man he was seeking—suggested
a mysterious similitude to the young fellow he had
distrusted and disliked from the first.

However that might have been, the silence was not
very prolonged. He took another oblique step.

"I reckon I had no more than a two-mile pull to
your ship. Not a bit more."

"And quite enough, too, in this awful heat," I said.

Another pause full of mistrust followed. Necessity,
they say, is mother of invention, but fear, too, is not
barren of ingenious suggestions. And I was afraid he
would ask me point-blank for news of my other self.

"Nice little saloon, isn't it?" I remarked, as if noticing for the first time the way his eyes roamed from
one closed door to the other. "And very well fitted
out, too. Here, for instance," I continued, reaching
over the back of my seat negligently and flinging the
door open, "is my bathroom."

He made an eager movement, but hardly gave it a
glance. I got up, shut the door of the bathroom, and
invited him to have a look round, as if I were very
proud of my accommodation. He had to rise and be

shown round, but he went through the business without any raptures whatever.

"And now we'll have a look at my stateroom," I declared, in a voice as loud as I dared to make it, crossing the cabin to the starboard side with purposely heavy steps.

He followed me in and gazed around. My intelligent double had vanished. I played my part.

"Very convenient—isn't it?"

"Very nice. Very comf . . ." He didn't finish and went out brusquely as if to escape from some unrighteous wiles of mine. But it was not to be. I had been too frightened not to feel vengeful; I felt I had him on the run, and I meant to keep him on the run. My polite insistence must have had something menacing in it, because he gave in suddenly. And I did not let him off a single item; mate's room, pantry, storerooms, the very sail locker which was also under the poop—he had to look into them all. When at last I showed him out on the quarter-deck he drew a long, spiritless sigh, and mumbled dismally that he must really be going back to his ship now. I desired my mate, who had joined us, to see to the captain's boat.

The man of whiskers gave a blast on the whistle which he used to wear hanging round his neck, and yelled, "*Sephora's* away!" My double down there in my cabin must have heard, and certainly could not feel more relieved than I. Four fellows came running out from somewhere forward and went over the side, while my own men, appearing on deck too, lined the rail. I escorted my visitor to the gangway ceremoniously, and nearly overdid it. He was a tenacious beast. On the very ladder he lingered, and in that unique, guiltily conscientious manner of sticking to the point:

"I say . . . you . . . you don't think that——"

I covered his voice loudly:

"Certainly not. . . . I am delighted. Good-by."

I had an idea of what he meant to say, and just saved myself by the privilege of defective hearing. He was too shaken generally to insist, but my mate, close witness of that parting, looked mystified and his face took on a thoughtful cast. As I did not want to appear as if I wished to avoid all communication with my officers, he had the opportunity to address me.

"Seems a very nice man. His boat's crew told our chaps a very extraordinary story, if what I am told by the steward is true. I suppose you had it from the captain, sir?"

"Yes. I had a story from the captain."

"A very horrible affair—isn't it, sir?"

"It is."

"Beats all these tales we hear about murders in Yankee ships."

"I don't think it beats them. I don't think it resembles them in the least."

"Bless my soul—you don't say so! But of course I've no acquaintance whatever with American ships, not I, so I couldn't go against your knowledge. It's horrible enough for me. . . . But the queerest part is that those fellows seemed to have some idea the man was hidden aboard here. They had really. Did you ever hear of such a thing?"

"Preposterous—isn't it?"

We were walking to and fro athwart the quarter-deck. No one of the crew forward could be seen (the day was Sunday), and the mate pursued:

"There was some little dispute about it. Our chaps took offense. 'As if we would harbor a thing like that,' they said. 'Wouldn't you like to look for him in our coal-hole?' Quite a tiff. But they made it up in the end. I suppose he did drown himself. Don't you, sir?"

"I don't suppose anything."

"You have no doubt in the matter, sir?"

"None whatever."

I left him suddenly. I felt I was producing a bad impression, but with my double down there it was most trying to be on deck. And it was almost as trying to be below. Altogether a nerve-trying situation. But on the whole I felt less torn in two when I was with him. There was no one in the whole ship whom I dared take into my confidence. Since the hands had got to know his story, it would have been impossible to pass him off for anyone else, and an accidental discovery was to be dreaded now more than ever. . . .

The steward being engaged in laying the table for dinner, we could talk only with our eyes when I first went down. Later in the afternoon we had a cautious try at whispering. The Sunday quietness of the ship was against us; the stillness of air and water around her was against us; the elements, the men were against us—everything was against us in our secret partnership; time itself—for this could not go on forever. The very trust in Providence was, I suppose, denied to his guilt. Shall I confess that this thought cast me down very much? And as to the chapter of accidents which counts for so much in the book of success, I could only hope that it was closed. For what favorable accident could be expected?

"Did you hear everything?" were my first words as soon as we took up our position side by side, leaning over my bed place.

He had. And the proof of it was his earnest whisper, "The man told you he hardly dared to give the order."

I understood the reference to be to that saving foresail.

"Yes. He was afraid of it being lost in the setting."

"I assure you he never gave the order. He may think he did, but he never gave it. He stood there with me on the break of the poop after the main topsail blew away, and whimpered about our last hope—positively whimpered about it and nothing else—and the night coming on! To hear one's skipper go on like that in such weather was enough to drive any fellow out of his mind. It worked me up into a sort of desperation. I just took it into my own hands and went away from him, boiling, and—— But what's the use telling you? *You* know! . . . Do you think that if I had not been pretty fierce with them I should have got the men to do anything? Not I! The bo's'n perhaps? Perhaps! It wasn't a heavy sea—it was a sea gone mad! I suppose the end of the world will be something like that; and a man may have the heart to see it coming once and be done with it—but to have to face it day

after day—— I don't blame anybody. I was precious
little better than the rest. Only—I was an officer of
that old coal wagon, anyhow——"

"I quite understand," I conveyed that sincere assurance into his ear. He was out of breath with whispering; I could hear him pant slightly. It was all very
simple. The same strung-up force which had given
twenty-four men a chance, at least, for their lives, had,
in a sort of recoil, crushed an unworthy mutinous
existence.

But I had no leisure to weigh the merits of the
matter—footsteps in the saloon, a heavy knock.
"There's enough wind to get under way with, sir."
Here was the call of a new claim upon my thoughts
and even upon my feelings.

"Turn the hands up," I cried through the door. "I'll
be on deck directly."

I was going out to make the acquaintance of my
ship. Before I left the cabin our eyes met—the eyes
of the only two strangers on board. I pointed to the
recessed part where the little campstool awaited him
and laid my finger on my lips. He made a gesture—
somewhat vague—a little mysterious, accompanied by
a faint smile, as if of regret.

This is not the place to enlarge upon the sensations
of a man who feels for the first time a ship move
under his feet to his own independent word. In my
case they were not unalloyed. I was not wholly alone
with my command; for there was that stranger in my
cabin. Or rather, I was not completely and wholly with
her. Part of me was absent. That mental feeling of
being in two places at once affected me physically as
if the mood of secrecy had penetrated my very soul.
Before an hour had elapsed since the ship had begun
to move, having occasion to ask the mate (he stood
by my side) to take a compass bearing of the pagoda,
I caught myself reaching up to his ears in whispers. I
say I caught myself, but enough had escaped to startle
the man. I can't describe it otherwise than by saying
that he shied. A grave, preoccupied manner, as though
he were in possession of some perplexing intelligence,

did not leave him henceforth. A little later I moved away from the rail to look at the compass with such a stealthy gait that the helmsman noticed it—and I could not help noticing the unusual roundness of his eyes. These are trifling instances, though it's to no commander's advantage to be suspected of ludicrous eccentricities. But I was also more seriously affected. There are to a seaman certain words, gestures, that should in given conditions come as naturally, as instinctively as the winking of a menaced eye. A certain order should spring on to his lips without thinking; a certain sign should get itself made, so to speak, without reflection. But all unconscious alertness had abandoned me. I had to make an effort of will to recall myself back (from the cabin) to the conditions of the moment. I felt that I was appearing an irresolute commander to those people who were watching me more or less critically.

And, besides, there were the scares. On the second day out, for instance, coming off the deck in the afternoon (I had straw slippers on my bare feet) I stopped at the open pantry door and spoke to the steward. He was doing something there with his back to me. At the sound of my voice he nearly jumped out of his skin, as the saying is, and incidentally broke a cup.

"What on earth's the matter with you?" I asked, astonished.

He was extremely confused. "Beg your pardon, sir. I made sure you were in your cabin."

"You see I wasn't."

"No, sir. I could have sworn I had heard you moving in there not a moment ago. It's most extraordinary . . . very sorry, sir."

I passed on with an inward shudder. I was so identified with my secret double that I did not even mention the fact in those scanty, fearful whispers we exchanged. I suppose he had made some slight noise of some kind or other. It would have been miraculous if he hadn't at one time or another. And yet, haggard as he appeared, he looked always perfectly self-controlled, more than calm—almost invulnerable. On my

suggestion he remained almost entirely in the bathroom, which, upon the whole, was the safest place.
There could be really no shadow of an excuse for
anyone ever wanting to go in there, once the steward
had done with it. It was a very tiny place. Sometimes
he reclined on the floor, his legs bent, his head sustained on one elbow. At others I would find him on
the campstool, sitting in his gray sleeping suit and with
his cropped dark hair like a patient, unmoved convict.
At night I would smuggle him into my bed place, and
we would whisper together, with the regular footfalls
of the officer of the watch passing and repassing over
our heads. It was an infinitely miserable time. It was
lucky that some tins of fine preserves were stowed in
a locker in my stateroom; hard bread I could always
get hold of; and so he lived on stewed chicken, *pâté
de foie gras,* asparagus, cooked oysters, sardines—on
all sorts of abominable sham delicacies out of tins. My
early-morning coffee he always drank; and it was all
I dared do for him in that respect.

Every day there was the horrible maneuvering to
go through so that my room and then the bathroom
should be done in the usual way. I came to hate the
sight of the steward, to abhor the voice of that harmless man. I felt that it was he who would bring on
the disaster of discovery. It hung like a sword over
our heads.

The fourth day out, I think (we were then working
down the east side of the Gulf of Siam, tack for tack,
in light winds and smooth water)—the fourth day, I
say, of this miserable juggling with the unavoidable, as
we sat at our evening meal, that man, whose slightest
movement I dreaded, after putting down the dishes
ran up on deck busily. This could not be dangerous.
Presently he came down again; and then it appeared
that he had remembered a coat of mine which I had
thrown over a rail to dry after having been wetted in
a shower which had passed over the ship in the afternoon. Sitting stolidly at the head of the table I became
terrified at the sight of the garment on his arm. Of

course he made for my door. There was no time to lose.

"Steward," I thundered. My nerves were so shaken that I could not govern my voice and conceal my agitation. This was the sort of thing that made my terrifically whiskered mate tap his forehead with his forefinger. I had detected him using that gesture while talking on deck with a confidential air to the carpenter. It was too far to hear a word, but I had no doubt that this pantomime could only refer to the strange new captain.

"Yes, sir," the pale-faced steward turned resignedly to me. It was this maddening course of being shouted at, checked without rhyme or reason, arbitrarily chased out of my cabin, suddenly called into it, sent flying out of his pantry on incomprehensible errands, that accounted for the growing wretchedness of his expression.

"Where are you going with that coat?"

"To your room, sir."

"Is there another shower coming?"

"I'm sure I don't know, sir. Shall I go up again and see, sir?"

"No! never mind."

My object was attained, as of course my other self in there would have heard everything that passed. During this interlude my two officers never raised their eyes off their respective plates; but the lip of that confounded cub, the second mate, quivered visibly.

I expected the steward to hook my coat on and come out at once. He was very slow about it; but I dominated my nervousness sufficiently not to shout after him. Suddenly I became aware (it could be heard plainly enough) that the fellow for some reason or other was opening the door of the bathroom. It was the end. The place was literally not big enough to swing a cat in. My voice died in my throat and I went stony all over. I expected to hear a yell of surprise and terror, and made a movement, but had not the strength to get on my legs. Everything remained still. Had my second self taken the poor wretch by the throat? I don't know what I could have done next moment if I had not seen the steward come out of my room, close the door, and then stand quietly by the sideboard.

"Saved," I thought. "But, no! Lost! Gone! He was gone!"

I laid my knife and fork down and leaned back in my chair. My head swam. After a while, when sufficiently recovered to speak in a steady voice, I instructed my mate to put the ship round at eight o'clock himself.

"I won't come on deck," I went on. "I think I'll turn in, and unless the wind shifts I don't want to be disturbed before midnight. I feel a bit seedy."

"You did look middling bad a little while ago," the chief mate remarked without showing any great concern.

They both went out, and I stared at the steward clearing the table. There was nothing to be read on that wretched man's face. But why did he avoid my eyes, I asked myself. Then I thought I should like to hear the sound of his voice.

"Steward!"

"Sir!" Startled as usual.

"Where did you hang up that coat?"

"In the bathroom, sir." The usual anxious tone. "It's not quite dry yet, sir."

For some time longer I sat in the cuddy. Had my double vanished as he had come? But of his comng there was an explanation, whereas his disappearance would be inexplicable. . . . I went slowly into my dark room, shut the door, lighted the lamp, and for a time dared not turn round. When at last I did I saw him standing bolt-upright in the narrow recessed part. It would not be true to say I had a shock, but an irresistible doubt of his bodily existence flitted through my mind. Can it be, I asked myself, that he is not visible to other eyes than mine? It was like being haunted. Motionless, with a grave face, he raised his hands slightly at me in a gesture which meant clearly, "Heavens! what a narrow escape!" Narrow indeed. I think

I had come creeping quietly as near insanity as any man who has not actually gone over the border. That gesture restrained me, so to speak.

The mate with the terrific whiskers was not putting the ship on the other tack. In the moment of profound silence which follows upon the hands going to their stations I heard on the poop his raised voice: "Hard alee!" and the distant shout of the order repeated on the main-deck. The sails, in that light breeze, made but a faint fluttering noise. It ceased. The ship was coming round slowly: I held my breath in the renewed stillness of expectation; one wouldn't have thought that there was a single living soul on her decks. A sudden brisk shout, "Mainsail haul!" broke the spell, and in the noisy cries and rush overhead of the men running away with the main brace we two, down in my cabin, came together in our usual position by the bed place.

He did not wait for my question. "I heard him fumbling here and just managed to squat myself down in the bath," he whispered to me. "The fellow only opened the door and put his arm in to hang the coat up. All the same——"

"I never thought of that," I whispered back, even more appalled than before at the closeness of the shave, and marveling at that something unyielding in his character which was carrying him through so finely. There was no agitation in his whisper. Whoever was being driven distracted, it was not he. He was sane. And the proof of his sanity was continued when he took up the whispering again.

"It would never do for me to come to life again."

It was something that a ghost might have said. But what he was alluding to was his old captain's reluctant admission of the theory of suicide. It would obviously serve his turn—if I had understood at all the view which seemed to govern the unalterable purpose of his action.

"You must maroon me as soon as ever you can get amongst these islands off the Cambodge shore," he went on.

"Maroon you! We are not living in a boy's adventure tale," I protested. His scornful whispering took me up.

"We aren't indeed! There's nothing of a boy's tale in this. But there's nothing else for it. I want no more. You don't suppose I am afraid of what can be done to me? Prison or gallows or whatever they may please. But you don't see me coming back to explain such things to an old fellow in a wig and twelve respectable tradesmen, do you? What can they know whether I am guilty or not—or of *what* I am guilty, either? That's my affair. What does the Bible say? 'Driven off the face of the earth.' Very well, I am off the face of the earth now. As I came at night so I shall go."

"Impossible!" I murmured. "You can't."

"Can't? . . . Not naked like a soul on the Day of Judgment. I shall freeze on to this sleeping suit. The Last Day is not yet—and . . . you have understood thoroughly. Didn't you?"

I felt suddenly ashamed of myself. I may say truly that I understood—and my hesitation in letting that man swim away from my ship's side had been a mere sham sentiment, a sort of cowardice.

"It can't be done now till next night," I breathed out. "The ship is on the off-shore tack and the wind may fail us."

"As long as I know that you understand," he whispered. "But of course you do. It's a great satisfaction to have got somebody to understand. You seem to have been there on purpose." And in the same whisper, as if we two whenever we talked had to say things to each other which were not fit for the world to hear, he added, "It's very wonderful."

We remained side by side talking in our secret way—but sometimes silent or just exchanging a whispered word or two at long intervals. And as usual he stared through the port. A breath of wind came now and again into our faces. The ship might have been moored in dock, so gently and on an even keel she slipped through the water, that did not murmur even at our passage, shàdowy and silent like a phantom sea.

At midnight I went on deck, and to my mate's great surprise put the ship round on the other tack. His terrible whiskers flitted round me in silent criticism. I certainly should not have done it if it had been only a question of getting out of that sleepy gulf as quickly as possible. I believe he told the second mate, who relieved him, that it was a great want of judgment. The other only yawned. That intolerable cub shuffled about so sleepily and lolled against the rails in such a slack, improper fashion that I came down on him sharply.

"Aren't you properly awake yet?"

"Yes, sir! I am awake."

"Well, then, be good enough to hold yourself as if you were. And keep a lookout. If there's any current we'll be closing with some islands before daylight."

The east side of the gulf is fringed with islands, some solitary, others in groups. On the blue background of the high coast they seem to float on silvery patches of calm water, arid and gray, or dark green and rounded like clumps of evergreen bushes, with the larger ones, a mile or two long, showing the outlines of ridges, ribs of gray rock under the dank mantle of matted leafage. Unknown to trade, to travel, almost to geography, the manner of life they harbor is an unsolved secret. There must be villages—settlements of fishermen at least—on the largest of them, and some communication with the world is probably kept up by native craft. But all that forenoon, as we headed for them, fanned along by the faintest of breezes, I saw no sign of man or canoe in the field of the telescope I kept on pointing at the scattered group.

At noon I gave no orders for a change of course, and the mate's whiskers became much concerned and seemed to be offering themselves unduly to my notice. At last I said:

"I am going to stand right in. Quite in—as far as I can take her."

The stare of extreme surprise imparted an air of ferocity also to his eyes, and he looked truly terrific for a moment.

"We're not doing well in the middle of the gulf," I continued, casually. "I am going to look for the land breezes tonight."

"Bless my soul! Do you mean, sir, in the dark amongst the lot of all them islands and reefs and shoals?"

"Well—if there are any regular land breezes at all on this coast one must get close inshore to find them, mustn't one?"

"Bless my soul!" he exclaimed again under his breath. All that afternoon he wore a dreamy, contemplative appearance which in him was a mark of perplexity. After dinner I went into my stateroom as if I meant to take some rest. There we two bent our dark heads over a half-unrolled chart lying on my bed.

"There," I said. "It's got to be Koh-ring. I've been looking at it ever since sunrise. It has got two hills and a low point. It must be inhabited. And on the coast opposite there is what looks like the mouth of a biggish river—with some towns, no doubt, not far up. It's the best chance for you that I can see."

"Anything. Koh-ring let it be."

He looked thoughtfully at the chart as if surveying chances and distances from a lofty height—and following with his eyes his own figure wandering on the blank land of Cochin-China, and then passing off that piece of paper clean out of sight into uncharted regions. And it was as if the ship had two captains to plan her course for her. I had been so worried and restless running up and down that I had not had the patience to dress that day. I had remained in my sleeping suit, with straw slippers and a soft floppy hat. The closeness of the heat in the gulf had been most oppressive, and the crew were used to seeing me wandering in that airy attire.

"She will clear the south point as she heads now," I whispered into his ear. "Goodness only knows when, though, but certainly after dark. I'll edge her in to half a mile, as far as I may be able to judge in the dark——"

"Be careful," he murmured, warningly—and I realized suddenly that all my future, the only future for which I was fit, would perhaps go irretrievably to pieces in any mishap to my first command.

I could not stop a moment longer in the room. I motioned him to get out of sight and made my way on the poop. That unplayful cub had the watch. I walked up and down for a while thinking things out, then beckoned him over.

"Send a couple of hands to open the two quarter-deck ports," I said, mildly.

He actually had the impudence, or else so forgot himself in his wonder at such an incomprehensible order, as to repeat:

"Open the quarter-deck ports! What for, sir?"

"The only reason you need concern yourself about is because I tell you to do so. Have them open wide and fastened properly."

He reddened and went off, but I believe made some jeering remark to the carpenter as to the sensible practice of ventilating a ship's quarter-deck. I know he popped into the mate's cabin to impart the fact to him because the whiskers came on deck, as it were by chance, and stole glances at me from below—for signs of lunacy or drunkenness, I suppose.

A little before supper, feeling more restless than ever, I rejoined, for a moment, my second self. And to find him sitting so quietly was surprising, like something against nature, inhuman.

I developed my plan in a hurried whisper.

"I shall stand in as close as I dare and then put her round. I will presently find means to smuggle you out of here into the sail locker, which communicates with the lobby. But there is an opening, a sort of square for hauling the sails out, which gives straight on the quarter-deck and which is never closed in fine weather, so as to give air to the sails. When the ship's way is deadened in stays and all the hands are aft at the main braces you will have a clear road to slip out and get overboard through the open quarter-deck port. I've had them both fastened up. Use a rope's end to lower yourself into the water so as to avoid a splash—you know. It could be heard and cause some beastly complication."

He kept silent for a while, then whispered, "I understand."

"I won't be there to see you go," I began with an effort. "The rest . . . I only hope I have understood, too."

"You have. From first to last"—and for the first time there seemed to be a faltering, something strained in his whisper. He caught hold of my arm, but the ringing of the supper bell made me start. He didn't though; he only released his grip.

After supper I didn't come below again till well past eight o'clock. The faint, steady breeze was loaded with dew; and the wet, darkened sails held all there was of propelling power in it. The night, clear and starry, sparkled darkly, and the opaque, lightless patches shifting slowly against the low stars were the drifting islets. On the port bow there was a big one more distant and shadowily imposing by the great space of sky it eclipsed.

On opening the door I had a back view of my very own self looking at a chart. He had come out of the recess and was standing near the table.

"Quite dark enough," I whispered.

He stepped back and leaned against my bed with a level, quiet glance. I sat on the couch. We had nothing to say to each other. Over our heads the officer of the watch moved here and there. Then I heard him move quickly. I knew what that meant. He was making for the companion; and presently his voice was outside my door.

"We are drawing in pretty fast, sir. Land looks rather close."

"Very well," I answered. "I am coming on deck directly."

I waited till he was gone out of the cuddy, then rose. My double moved too. The time had come to exchange our last whispers, for neither of us was ever to hear each other's natural voice.

"Look here!" I opened a drawer and took out three

sovereigns. "Take this anyhow. I've got six and I'd give you the lot, only I must keep a little money to buy some fruit and vegetables for the crew from native boats as we go through Sunda Straits."

He shook his head.

"Take it," I urged him, whispering desperately. "No one can tell what——"

He smiled and slapped meaningly the only pocket of the sleeping jacket. It was not safe, certainly. But I produced a large old silk handkerchief of mine, and tying the three pieces of gold in a corner, pressed it on him. He was touched, I supposed, because he took it at last and tied it quickly round his waist under the jacket, on his bare skin.

Our eyes met; several seconds elapsed, till, our glances still mingled, I extended my hand and turned the lamp out. Then I passed through the cuddy, leaving the door of my room wide open. . . . "Steward!"

He was still lingering in the pantry in the greatness of his zeal, giving a rub-up to a plated cruet stand the last thing before going to bed. Being careful not to wake up the mate, whose room was opposite, I spoke in an undertone.

He looked round anxiously. "Sir!"

"Can you get me a little hot water from the galley?"

"I am afraid, sir, the galley fire's been out for some time now."

"Go and see."

He flew up the stairs.

"Now," I whispered, loudly, into the saloon—too loudly, perhaps, but I was afraid I couldn't make a sound. He was by my side in an instant—the double captain slipped past the stairs—through a tiny dark passage . . . a sliding door. We were in the sail locker, scrambling on our knees over the sails. A sudden thought struck me. I saw myself wandering barefooted, bareheaded, the sun beating on my dark poll. I snatched off my floppy hat and tried hurriedly in the dark to ram it on my other self. He dodged and fended off silently. I wonder what he thought had come to me before he understood and suddenly desisted. Our hands met gropingly, lingered united in a steady, motionless clasp for a second. . . . No word was breathed by either of us when they separated.

I was standing quietly by the pantry door when the steward returned.

"Sorry, sir. Kettle barely warm. Shall I light the spirit lamp?"

"Never mind."

I came out on deck slowly. It was now a matter of conscience to shave the land as close as possible—for now he must go overboard whenever the ship was put in stays. Must! There could be no going back for him. After a moment I walked over to leeward and my heart flew into my mouth at the nearness of the land on the bow. Under any other circumstances I would not have held on a minute longer. The second mate had followed me anxiously.

I looked on till I felt I could command my voice.

"She will weather," I said then in a quiet tone.

"Are you going to try that, sir?" he stammered out incredulously.

I took no notice of him and raised my tone just enough to be heard by the helmsman.

"Keep her good full."

"Good full, sir."

The wind fanned my cheek, the sails slept, the world was silent. The strain of watching the dark loom of the land grow bigger and denser was too much for me. I had shut my eyes—because the ship must go closer. She must! The stillness was intolerable. Were we standing still?

When I opened my eyes the second view started my heart with a thump. The black southern hill of Kohring seemed to hang right over the ship like a towering fragment of the ever-lasting night. On that enormous mass of blackness there was not a gleam to be seen, not a sound to be heard. It was gliding irresistibly towards us and yet seemed already within reach of the hand. I saw the vague figures of the watch grouped in the waist, gazing in awed silence.

"Are you going on, sir?" inquired an unsteady voice at my elbow.

I ignored it. I had to go on.

"Keep her full. Don't check her way. That won't do now," I said, warningly.

"I can't see the sails very well," the helmsman answered me, in strange, quavering tones.

Was she close enough? Already she was, I won't say in the shadow of the land, but in the very blackness of it, already swallowed up as it were, gone too close to be recalled, gone from me altogether.

"Give the mate a call," I said to the young man who stood at my elbow as still as death. "And turn all hands up."

My tone had a borrowed loudness reverberated from the height of the land. Several voices cried out together: "We are all on deck, sir."

Then stillness again, with the great shadow gliding closer, towering higher, without a light, without a sound. Such a hush had fallen on the ship that she might have been a bark of the dead floating in slowly under the very gate of Erebus.

"My God! Where are we?"

It was the mate moaning at my elbow. He was thunder-struck, and as it were deprived of the moral support of his whiskers. He clapped his hands and absolutely cried out, "Lost!"

"Be quiet," I said, sternly.

He lowered his tone, but I saw the shadowy gesture of his despair. "What are we doing here?"

"Looking for the land wind."

He made as if to tear his hair, and addressed me recklessly.

"She will never get out. You have done it, sir. I knew it'd end in something like this. She will never weather, and you are too close now to stay. She'll drift ashore before she's round. O my God!"

I caught his arm as he was raising it to batter his poor devoted head, and shook it violently.

"She's ashore already," he wailed, trying to tear himself away.

"Is she? . . . Keep good full there!"

"Good full, sir," cried the helmsman in a frightened, thin, childlike voice.

I hadn't let go the mate's arm and went on shaking it. "Ready about, do you hear? You go forward"—shake—"and stop there"—shake—"and hold your noise"—shake—"and see these head-sheets properly overhauled"—shake, shake—shake.

And all the time I dared not look towards the land lest my heart should fail me. I released my grip at last and he ran forward as if fleeing for dear life.

I wondered what my double there in the sail locker thought of this commotion. He was able to hear everything—and perhaps he was able to understand why, on my conscience, it had to be thus close—no less. My first order "Hard alee!" re-echoed ominously under the towering shadow of Koh-ring as if I had shouted in a mountain gorge. And then I watched the land intently. In that smooth water and light wind it was impossible to feel the ship coming-to. No! I could not feel her. And my second self was making now ready to ship out and lower himself overboard. Perhaps he was gone already . . . ?

The great black mass brooding over our very mastheads began to pivot away from the ship's side silently. And now I forgot the secret stranger ready to depart, and remembered only that I was a total stranger to the ship. I did not know her. Would she do it? How was she to be handled?

I swung the mainyard and waited helplessly. She was perhaps stopped, and her very fate hung in the balance, with the black mass of Koh-ring like the gate of the everlasting night towering over her taffrail. What would she do now? Had she way on her yet? I stepped to the side swiftly, and on the shadowy water I could see nothing except a faint phosphorescent flash revealing the glassy smoothness of the sleeping surface. It was impossible to tell—and I had not learned yet the feel of my ship. Was she moving? What I needed was something easily seen, a piece of paper, which I could throw overboard and watch. I had noth-

ing on me. To run down for it I didn't dare. There
was no time. All at once my strained, yearning stare
distinguished a white object floating within a yard of
the ship's side. White on the black water. A phosphorescent flash passed under it. What was that thing? . . .
I recognized my own floppy hat. It must have fallen
off his head . . . and he didn't bother. Now I had what
I wanted—the saving mark for my eyes. But I hardly
thought of my other self, now gone from the ship, to
be hidden forever from all friendly faces, to be a fugitive and a vagabond on the earth, with no brand of
the curse on his sane forehead to stay a slaying
hand . . . too proud to explain.

And I watched the hat—the expression of my sudden pity for his mere flesh. It had been meant to save
his homeless head from the dangers of the sun. And
now—behold—it was saving the ship, by serving me
for a mark to help out the ignorance of my strangeness. Ha! It was drifting forward, warning me just in
time that the ship had gathered sternway.

"Shift the helm," I said in a low voice to the seaman
standing still like a statue.

The man's eyes glistened wildly in the binnacle light
as he jumped round to the other side and spun round
the wheel.

I walked to the break of the poop. On the over-
shadowed deck all hands stood by the forebraces waiting for my order. The stars ahead seemed to be gliding
from right to left. And all was so still in the world
that I heard the quiet remark, "She's round," passed
in a tone of intense relief between two seamen.

"Let go and haul."

The foreyards ran round with a great noise, amidst
cheery cries. And now the frightful whiskers made
themselves heard giving various orders. Already the
ship was drawing ahead. And I was alone with her.
Nothing! no one in the world should stand now between us, throwing a shadow on the way of silent
knowledge and mute affection, the perfect communion
of a seaman with his first command.

Walking to the taffrail, I was in time to make out,

on the very edge of a darkness thrown by a towering black mass like the very gateway of Erebus—yes, I was in time to catch an evanescent glimpse of my white hat left behind to mark the spot where the secret sharer of my cabin and of my thoughts, as though he were my second self, had lowered himself into the water to take his punishment: a free man, a proud swimmer striking out for a new destiny.

Heart of Darkness

I

The *Nellie,* a cruising yawl, swung to her anchor without a flutter of the sails, and was at rest. The flood had made, the wind was nearly calm, and being bound down the river, the only thing for it was to come to and wait for the turn of the tide.

The sea-reach of the Thames stretched before us like the beginning of an interminable waterway. In the offing the sea and the sky were welded together without a joint, and in the luminous space the tanned sails of the barges drifting up with the tide seemed to stand still in red clusters of canvas sharply peaked, with gleams of varnished sprits. A haze rested on the low shores that ran out to sea in vanishing flatness. The air was dark above Gravesend, and farther back still seemed condensed into a mournful gloom, brooding motionless over the biggest, and the greatest, town on earth.

The Director of Companies was our captain and our host. We four affectionately watched his back as he stood in the bows looking to seaward. On the whole river there was nothing that looked half so nautical. He resembled a pilot, which to a seaman is trustworthiness personified. It was difficult to realize his work was not out there in the luminous estuary, but behind him, within the brooding gloom.

Between us there was, as I have already said somewhere, the bond of the sea. Besides holding our hearts together through long periods of separation, it had the effect of making us tolerant of each other's yarns— and even convictions. The Lawyer—the best of old fellows—had, because of his many years and many virtues, the only cushion on deck, and was lying on the only rug. The Accountant had brought out already a box of dominoes, and was toying architecturally with the bones. Marlow sat cross-legged right aft, leaning against the mizzen-mast. He had sunken cheeks, a yellow complexion, a straight back, an ascetic aspect, and, with his arms dropped, the palms of hands outwards, resembled an idol. The director, satisfied the anchor had good hold, made his way aft and sat down amongst us. We exchanged a few words lazily. Afterwards there was silence on board the yacht. For some reason or other we did not begin that game of dominoes. We felt meditative, and fit for nothing but placid staring. The day was ending in a serenity of still and exquisite brilliance. The water shone pacifically; the sky, without a speck, was a benign immensity of unstained light; the very mist on the Essex marsh was like a gauzy and radiant fabric, hung from the wooded rises inland, and draping the low shores in diaphanous folds. Only the gloom to the west, brooding over the upper reaches, became more sombre every minute, as if angered by the approach of the sun.

And at last, in its curved and imperceptible fall, the sun sank low, and from glowing white changed to a dull red without rays and without heat, as if about to go out suddenly, stricken to death by the touch of that gloom brooding over a crowd of men.

Forthwith a change came over the waters, and the serenity became less brilliant but more profound. The old river in its broad reach rested unruffled at the decline of day, after ages of good service done to the race that peopled its banks, spread out in the tranquil dignity of a waterway leading to the uttermost ends of the earth. We looked at the venerable stream not in the vivid flush of a short day that comes and departs for ever, but in the august light of abiding memories. And indeed nothing is easier for a man who has, as the phrase goes, "followed the sea" with reverence and affection, than to evoke the great spirit of the past upon the lower reaches of the Thames. The tidal current runs to and fro in its unceasing service,

crowded with memories of men and ships it had borne
to the rest of home or to the battles of the sea. It had
known and served all the men of whom the nation is
proud, from Sir Francis Drake to Sir John Franklin,
knights all, titled and untitled—the great knights-
errant of the sea. It had borne all the ships whose
names are like jewels flashing in the night of time,
from the *Golden Hind* returning with her round flanks
full of treasure, to be visited by the Queen's Highness
and thus pass out of the gigantic tale, to the *Erebus*
and *Terror,* bound on other conquests—and that never
returned. It had known the ships and the men. They
had sailed from Deptford, from Greenwich, from
Erith—the adventurers and the settlers; kings' ships
and the ships of men on 'Change; captains, admirals,
the dark "interlopers" of the Eastern trade, and the
commissioned "generals" of East India fleets. Hunters
for gold or pursuers of fame, they all had gone out
on that stream, bearing the sword, and often the torch,
messengers of the might within the land, bearers of a
spark from the sacred fire. What greatness had not
floated on the ebb of that river into the mystery of an
unknown earth! . . . The dreams of men, the seed of
commonwealths, the germs of empires.

The sun set; the dusk fell on the stream, and lights
began to appear along the shore. The Chapman light-
house, a three-legged thing erect on a mud-flat, shone
strongly. Lights of ships moved in the fairway—a great
stir of lights going up and going down. And further
west on the upper reaches the place of the monstrous
town was still marked ominously on the sky, a brooding gloom in sunshine, a lurid glare under the stars.

"And this also," said Marlow suddenly, "has been
one of the dark places of the earth."

He was the only man of us who still "followed the
sea." The worst that could be said of him was that he
did not represent his class. He was a seaman, but he
was a wanderer, too, while most seamen lead, if one
may so express it, a sedentary life. Their minds are of
the stay-at-home order, and their home is always with
them—the ship; and so is their country—the sea. One

ship is very much like another, and the sea is always
the same. In the immutability of their surroundings
the foreign shores, the foreign faces, the changing immensity of life, glide past, veiled not by a sense of
mystery but by a slightly disdainful ignorance; for
there is nothing mysterious to a seaman unless it be
the sea itself, which is the mistress of his existence
and as inscrutable as Destiny. For the rest, after his
hours of work, a casual stroll or a casual spree of
shore suffices to unfold for him the secret of a whole
continent, and generally he finds the secret not worth
knowing. The yarns of seamen have a direct simplicity,
the whole meaning of which lies within the shell of a
cracked nut. But Marlow was not typical (if his propensity to spin yards be excepted), and to him the
meaning of an episode was not inside like a kernel
but outside, enveloping the tale which brought it out
only as a glow brings out a haze, in the likeness of
one of these misty halos that sometimes are made visible by the spectral illumination of moonshine.

His remark did not seem at all surprising. It was
just like Marlow. It was accepted in silence. No one
took the trouble to grunt even; and presently he said,
very slow—

"I was thinking of very old times, when the Romans
first came here, nineteen hundred years ago—the
other day. . . . Light came out of this river since—you
say Knights? Yes; but it is like a running blaze on a
plain, like a flash of lightning in the clouds. We live
in the flicker—may it last as long as the old earth
keeps rolling! But darkness was here yesterday. Imagine the feelings of a commander of a fine—what d'ye
call 'em?—trireme in the Mediterranean, ordered suddenly to the north; run overland across the Gauls in
a hurry; put in charge of one of these craft the legion-
aries—a wonderful lot of handy men they must have
been, too—used to build, apparently by the hundred,
in a month or two, if we may believe what we read.
Imagine him here—the very end of the world, a sea
the colour of lead, a sky the colour of smoke, a kind
of ship about as rigid as a concertina—and going up

this river with stores, or orders, or what you like. Sand-banks, marshes, forests, savages,—precious little to eat fit for a civilized man, nothing but Thames water to drink. No Falernian wine here, no going ashore. Here and there a military camp lost in the wilderness, like a needle in a bundle of hay—cold, fog, tempests, disease, exile, and death—death skulking in the air, in the water, in the bush. They must have been dying like flies here. Oh, yes—he did it. Did it very well, too, no doubt, and without thinking much about it either, except afterwards to brag of what he had gone through in his time, perhaps. They were men enough to face the darkness. And perhaps he was cheered by keeping his eye on a chance of promotion to the fleet at Ravenna by and by, if he had good friends in Rome and survived the awful climate. Or think of a decent young citizen in a toga—perhaps too much dice, you know—coming out here in the train of some prefect, or tax-gatherer, or trader even, to mend his fortunes. Land in a swamp, march through the woods, and in some inland post feel the savagery, the utter savagery, had closed round him—all that mysterious life of the wilderness that stirs in the forest, in the jungles, in the hearts of wild men. There's no initiation either into such mysteries. He has to live in the midst of the incomprehensible, which is also detestable. And it has a fascination, too, that goes to work upon him. The fascination of the abomination— you know, imagine the growing regrets, the longing to escape, the powerless disgust, the surrender, the hate."

He paused.

"Mind," he began again, lifting one arm from the elbow, the palm of the hand outwards, so that, with his legs folded before him, he had the pose of a Buddha preaching in European clothes and without a lotus-flower—"Mind, none of us would feel exactly like this. What saves us is efficiency—the devotion to efficiency. But these chaps were not much account, really. They were no colonists; their administration was merely a squeeze, and nothing more, I suspect. They were con-querors, and for that you want only brute force—nothing to boast of, when you have it, since your strength is just an accident arising from the weakness of others. They grabbed what they could get for the sake of what was to be got. It was just robbery with violence, aggravated murder on a great scale, and men going at it blind—as is very proper for those who tackle a darkness. The conquest of the earth, which mostly means the taking it away from those who have a different complexion or slightly flatter noses than ourselves, is not a pretty thing when you look into it too much. What redeems it is the idea only. An idea at the back of it; not a sentimental pretence but an idea; and an unselfish belief in the idea—something you can set up, and bow down before, and offer a sacrifice to. . . ."

He broke off. Flames glided in the river, small green flames, red flames, white flames, pursuing, overtaking, joining, crossing each other—then separating slowly or hastily. The traffic of the great city went on in the deepening night upon the sleepless river. We looked on, waiting patiently—there was nothing else to do till the end of the flood; but it was only after a long silence, when he said, in a hesitating voice, "I suppose you fellows remember I did once turn fresh-water sailor for a bit," that we knew we were fated, before the ebb began to run, to hear about one of Marlow's inconclusive experiences.

"I don't want to bother you much with what happened to me personally," he began, showing in this remark the weakness of many tellers of tales who seem so often unaware of what their audience would best like to hear; "yet to understand the effect of it on me you ought to know how I got out there, what I saw, how I went up that river to the place where I first met the poor chap. It was the farthest point of navigation and the culminating point of my experience. It seemed somehow to throw a kind of light on everything about me—and into my thoughts. It was sombre enough, too—and pitiful—not extraordinary in any way—not very clear either. No, not very clear. And yet it seemed to throw a kind of light.

"I had then, as you remember, just returned to Lon-

don after a lot of Indian Ocean, Pacific, China Seas—
a regular dose of the East—six years or so, and I was
loafing about, hindering you fellows in your work and
invading your homes, just as though I had got a heavenly mission to civilize you. It was very fine for a time,
but after a bit I did get tired of resting. Then I began
to look for a ship—I should think the hardest work
on earth. But the ships wouldn't even look at me. And
I got tired of that game, too.

"Now when I was a little chap I had a passion for
maps. I would look for hours at South America, or
Africa, or Australia, and lose myself in all the glories
of exploration. At that time there were many blank
spaces on the earth, and when I saw one that looked
particularly inviting on a map (but they all look that)
I would put my finger on it and say, 'When I grow up
I will go there.' The North Pole was one of these
places, I remember. Well, I haven't been there yet,
and shall not try now. The glamour's off. Other places
were scattered about the Equator, and in every sort
of latitude all over the two hemispheres. I have been
in some of them, and . . . well we won't talk about
that. But there was one yet—the biggest, the most
blank, so to speak—that I had a hankering after.

"True, by this time it was not a blank space any
more. It had got filled since my boyhood with rivers
and lakes and names. It had ceased to be a blank
space of delightful mystery—a white patch for a boy
to dream gloriously over. It had become a place of
darkness. But there was in it one river especially, a
mighty big river, that you could see on the map, resembling an immense snake uncoiled, with its head in
the sea, its body at rest curving afar over a vast country, and its tail lost in the depths of the land. And as
I looked at the map of it in a shop-window, it fascinated me as a snake would a bird—a silly little bird.
Then I remembered there was a big concern, a Company for trade on that river. Dash it all! I thought to
myself, they can't trade without using some kind of
craft on that lot of fresh water—steamboats! Why
shouldn't I try to get charge of one? I went on along

Fleet Street, but could not shake off the idea. The snake had charmed me.

"You understand it was a Continental concern, that Trading society; but I have a lot of relations living on the Continent, because it's cheap and not so nasty as it looks, they say.

"I am sorry to own I began to worry them. This was already a fresh departure for me. I was not used to get things that way, you know. I always went my own road and on my own legs where I had a mind to go. I wouldn't have believed it of myself; but, then—you see—I felt somehow I must get there by hook or by crook. So I worried them. The men said 'My dear fellow,' and did nothing. Then—would you believe it?—I tried the women. I, Charlie Marlow, set the women to work—to get a job. Heavens! Well, you see, the notion drove me. I had an aunt, a dear enthusiastic soul. She wrote: 'It will be delightful. I am ready to do anything, anything for you. It is a glorious idea. I know the wife of a very high personage in the Administration, and also a man who has lots of influence with,' etc., etc. She was determined to make no end of fuss to get me appointed skipper of a river steamboat, if such was my fancy.

"I got my appointment—of course; and I got it very quick. It appears the Company had received news that one of their captains had been killed in a scuffle with the natives. This was my chance, and it made me the more anxious to go. It was only months and months afterwards, when I made the attempt to recover what was left of the body, that I heard the original quarrel arose from a misunderstanding about some hens. Yes, two black hens. Fresleven—that was the fellow's name, a Dane—thought himself wronged somehow in the bargain, so he went ashore and started to hammer the chief of the village with a stick. Oh, it didn't surprise me in the least to hear this, and at the same time to be told that Fresleven was the gentlest, quietest creature that ever walked on two legs. No doubt he was; but he had been a couple of years already out there engaged in the noble cause, you know, and he probably felt the need at last of asserting his self-respect in some way. Therefore he whacked the old nigger mercilessly, while a big crowd of his people watched him, thunderstruck, till some man—I was told the chief's son—in desperation at hearing the old chap yell, made a tentative jab with a spear at the white man—and of course it went quite easy between the shoulderblades. Then the whole population cleared into the forest, expecting all kinds of calamities to happen, while, on the other hand, the steamer Fresleven commanded left also in a bad panic, in charge of the engineer, I believe. Afterwards nobody seemed to trouble much about Fresleven's remains, till I got out and stepped into his shoes. I couldn't let it rest, though; but when an opportunity offered at last to meet my predecessor, the grass growing through his ribs was tall enough to hide his bones. They were all there. The supernatural being had not been touched after he fell. And the village was deserted, the huts gaped black, rotting, all askew within the fallen enclosures. A calamity had come to it, sure enough. The people had vanished. Mad terror had scattered them, men, women, and children, through the bush, and they had never returned. What became of the hens I don't know either. I should think the cause of progress got them, anyhow. However, through this glorious affair I got my appointment, before I had fairly begun to hope for it.

"I flew around like mad to get ready, and before forty-eight hours I was crossing the Channel to show myself to my employers, and sign the contract. In a very few hours I arrived in a city that always makes me think of a whited sepulchre. Prejudice no doubt. I had no difficulty in finding the Company's offices. It was the biggest thing in the town, and everybody I met was full of it. They were going to run an oversea empire, and make no end of coin by trade.

"A narrow and deserted street in deep shadow, high houses, innumerable windows with venetian blinds, a dead silence, grass sprouting between the stones, imposing carriage archways right and left, immense double doors standing ponderously ajar. I slipped through one of these cracks, went up a swept and ungarnished staircase, as arid as a desert, and opened the first door I came to. Two women, one fat and the other slim, sat on straw-bottomed chairs, knitting black wool. The slim one got up and walked straight at me—still knitting with downcast eyes—and only just as I began to think of getting out of her way, as you would for a somnambulist, stood still, and looked up. Her dress was as plain as an umbrella-cover, and she turned round without a word and preceded me into a waiting-room. I gave my name, and looked about. Deal table in the middle, plain chairs all round the walls, on one end a large shining map, marked with all the colours of a rainbow. There was a vast amount of red—good to see at any time, because one knows that some real work is done in there, a deuce of a lot of blue, a little green, smears of orange, and, on the East Coast, a purple patch, to show where the jolly pioneers of progress drink the jolly lager-beer. However, I wasn't going into any of these. I was going into the yellow. Dead in the centre. And the river was there—fascinating—deadly—like a snake. Ough! A door opened, a white-haired secretarial head, but wearing a compassionate expression, appeared, and a skinny forefinger beckoned me into the sanctuary. Its light was dim, and a heavy writing-desk squatted in the middle. From behind that structure came out an impression of pale plumpness in a frock-coat. The great man himself. He was five feet six, I should judge, and had his grip on the handle-end of ever so many millions. He shook hands, I fancy, murmured vaguely, was satisfied with my French. *Bon voyage.*

"In about forty-five seconds I found myself again in the waiting-room with the compassionate secretary, who, full of desolation and sympathy, made me sign some document. I believe I undertook amongst other things not to disclose any trade secrets. Well, I am not going to.

"I began to feel slightly uneasy. You know I am not used to such ceremonies, and there was something ominous in the atmosphere. It was just as though I had been let into some conspiracy—I don't know— something not quite right; and I was glad to get out. In the outer room the two women knitted black wool feverishly. People were arriving, and the younger one was walking back and forth introducing them. The old one sat on her chair. Her flat cloth slippers were propped up on a foot-warmer, and a cat reposed on her lap. She wore a starched white affair on her head, had a wart on one cheek, and silver-rimmed spectacles hung on the top of her nose. She glanced at me above the glasses. The swift and indifferent placidity of that look troubled me. Two youths with foolish and cheery countenances were being piloted over, and she threw at them the same quick glance of unconcerned wisdom. She seemed to know all about them and about me, too. An eerie feeling came over me. She seemed uncanny and fateful. Often far away there I thought of these two, guarding the door of Darkness, knitting black wool as for a warm pall, one introducing, introducing continuously to the unknown, the other scrutinizing the cheery and foolish faces with unconcerned old eyes. *Ave!* Old knitter of black wool. *Morituri te salutant.* Not many of those she looked at ever saw her again—not half, by a long way.

"There was yet a visit to the doctor. 'A simple formality,' assured me the secretary, with an air of taking an immense part in all my sorrows. Accordingly a young chap wearing his hat over the left eyebrow, some clerk I suppose—there must have been clerks in the business, though the house was as still as a house in a city of the dead—came from somewhere up-stairs, and led me forth. He was shabby and careless, with inkstains on the sleeves of his jacket, and his cravat was large and billowy, under a chin shaped like the toe of an old boot. It was a little too early for the doctor, so I proposed a drink, and thereupon he developed a vein of joviality. As we sat over our vermouths he glorified the Company's business, and by and by I expressed casually my surprise at him not going out there. He became very cool and collected all at once.

'I am not such a fool as I look, quoth Plato to his disciples,' he said sententiously, emptied his glass with great resolution, and we rose.

"The old doctor felt my pulse, evidently thinking of something else the while. 'Good, good for there,' he mumbled, and then with a certain eagerness asked me whether I would let him measure my head. Rather surprised, I said Yes, when he produced a thing like calipers and got the dimensions back and front and every way, taking notes carefully. He was an unshaven little man in a threadbare coat like a gaberdine, with his feet in slippers, and I thought him a harmless fool. 'I always ask leave, in the interests of science, to measure the crania of those going out there,' he said. 'And when they come back, too?' I asked. 'Oh, I never see them,' he remarked; 'and, moreover, the changes take place inside, you know.' He smiled, as if at some quiet joke. 'So you are going out there. Famous. Interesting, too.' He gave me a searching glance, and made another note. 'Ever any madness in your family?' he asked, in a matter-of-fact tone. I felt very annoyed. 'Is that question in the interests of science, too?' 'It would be,' he said, without taking notice of my irritation, 'interesting for science to watch the mental changes of individuals, on the spot, but . . .' 'Are you an alienist?' I interrupted. 'Every doctor should be—a little,' answered that original, imperturbably. 'I have a little theory which you messieurs who go out there must help me to prove. This is my share in the advantages my country shall reap from the possession of such a magnificent dependency. The mere wealth I leave to others. Pardon my questions, but you are the first Englishman coming under my observation . . .' I hastened to assure him I was not in the least typical. 'If I were,' said I, 'I wouldn't be talking like this with you,' 'What you say is rather profound, and probably erroneous,' he said, with a laugh. 'Avoid irritation more than exposure to the sun. Adieu. How do you English say, eh? Good-bye. Ah! Good-bye. Adieu. In the tropics one must before everything keep calm.' . . . He lifted a warning forefinger. . . . 'Du calme, du calme. Adieu.'

"One thing more remained to do—say good-bye to my excellent aunt. I found her triumphant. I had a cup of tea—the last decent cup of tea for many days—and in a room that most soothingly looked just as you would expect a lady's drawing-room to look, we had a long quiet chat by the fireside. In the course of these confidences it became quite plain to me I had been represented to the wife of the high dignitary, and goodness knows to how many more people besides, as an exceptional and gifted creatures—a piece of good fortune for the Company—a man you don't get hold of every day. Good heavens! and I was going to take charge of a two-penny-half-penny river-steamboat with a penny whistle attached! It appeared, however, I was also one of the Workers, with a capital—you know. Something like an emissary of light, something like a lower sort of apostle. There had been a lot of such rot let loose in print and talk just about that time, and the excellent woman, living right in the rush of all that humbug, got carried off her feet. She talked about 'weaning those ignorant millions from their horrid ways,' till, upon my word, she made me quite uncomfortable. I ventured to hint that the Company was run for profit.

" 'You forget, dear Charlie, that the labourer is worthy of his hire,' she said, brightly. It's queer how out of touch with truth women are. They live in a world of their own, and there has never been anything like it, and never can be. It is too beautiful altogether, and if they were to set it up it would go to pieces before the first sunset. Some confounded fact we men have been living contentedly with ever since the day of creation would start up and knock the whole thing over.

"After this I got embraced, told to wear flannel, be sure to write often, and so on—and I left. In the street—I don't know why—a queer feeling came to me that I was an imposter. Odd thing that I, who used to clear out for any part of the world at twenty-four hours' notice, with less thought than most men give to the crossing of a street, had a moment—I won't say of hesitation, but of startled pause, before this

commonplace affair. The best way I can explain it to
you is by saying that, for a second or two, I felt as
though, instead of going to the centre of a continent,
I were about to set off for the centre of the earth.

"I left in a French steamer, and she called in every
blamed port they have out there, for, as far as I could
see, the sole purpose of landing soldiers and custom-
house officers. I watched the coast. Watching a coast
as its slips by the ship is like thinking about an enigma.
There it is before you—smiling, frowning, inviting,
grand, mean, insipid, or savage, and always mute with
an air of whispering, 'Come and find out.' This one
was almost featureless, as if still in the making, with an
aspect of monotonous grimness. The edge of a colossal
jungle, so dark-green as to be almost black, fringed
with white surf, ran straight, like a ruled line, far, far
away along a blue sea whose glitter was blurred by a
creeping mist. The sun was fierce, the land seemed to
glisten and drip with steam. Here and there greyish-
whitish specks showed up clustered inside the white
surf, with a flag flying above them perhaps. Settlements some centuries old, and still no bigger than pin-
heads on the untouched expanse of their background.
We pounded along, stopped, landed soldiers; went on,
landed custom-house clerks to levy toll in what looked
like a God-forsaken wilderness, with a tin shed and a
flag-pole lost in it; landed more soldiers—to take care
of the custom-house clerks, presumably. Some, I
heard, got drowned in the surf; but whether they did
or not, nobody seemed particularly to care. They were
just flung out there, and on we went. Every day the
coast looked the same, as though we had not moved;
but we passed various places—trading places—with
names like Gran' Bassam, Little Popo; names that
seemed to belong to some sordid farce acted in front
of a sinister back-cloth. The idleness of a passenger,
my isolation amongst all these men with whom I had
no point of contact, the oily and languid sea, the uniform sombreness of the coast, seemed to keep me
away from the truth of things, within the toil of a
mournful and senseless delusion. The voice of the surf

heard now and then was a positive pleasure, like the
speech of a brother. It was something natural, that
had its reason, that had a meaning. Now and then a
boat from the shore gave one a momentary contact
with reality. It was paddled by black fellows. You
could see from afar the white of their eyeballs glistening. They shouted, sang; their bodies streamed with
perspiration; they had faces like grotesque masks—
these chaps; but they had bone, muscle, a wild vitality,
an intense energy of movement, that was as natural
and true as the surf along their coast. They wanted
no excuse for being there. They were a great comfort
to look at. For a time I would feel I belonged still to
a world of straightforward facts; but the feeling would
not last long. Something would turn up to scare it
away. Once, I remember, we came upon a man-of-war
anchored off the coast. There wasn't even a shed
there, and she was shelling the bush. It appears the
French had one of their wars going on thereabouts.
Her ensign dropped limp like a rag; the muzzles of
the long six-inch guns stuck out all over the low hull;
the greasy, slimy swell swung her up lazily and let her
down, swaying her thin masts. In the empty immensity
of earth, sky, and water, there she was, incomprehensible, firing into a continent. Pop, would go one of the
six-inch guns; a small flame would dart and vanish, a
little white smoke would disappear, a tiny projectile
would give a feeble screech—and nothing happened.
Nothing could happen. There was a touch of insanity
in the proceeding, a sense of lugubrious drollery in
the sight; and it was not dissipated by somebody on
board assuring me earnestly there was a camp of natives—he called them enemies!—hidden out of sight
somewhere.

"We gave her her letters (I heard the men in that
lonely ship were dying of fever at the rate of three a
day) and went on. We called at some more places with
farcical names, where the merry dance of death and
trade goes on in a still and earthy atmosphere as of
an overheated catacomb; all along the formless coast
bordered by dangerous surf, as if Nature herself had

tried to ward off intruders; in and out of rivers, streams of death in life, whose banks were rotting into mud, whose waters, thickened into slime, invaded the contorted mangroves, that seemed to writhe at us in the extremity of an impotent despair. Nowhere did we stop long enough to get a particularized impression, but the general sense of vague and oppressive wonder grew upon me. It was like a weary pilgrimage amongst hints for nightmares.

"It was upward of thirty days before I saw the mouth of the big river. We anchored off the seat of the government. But my work would not begin till some two hundred miles farther on. So as soon as I could I made a start for a place thirty miles higher up.

"I had my passage on a little sea-going steamer. Her captain was a Swede, and knowing me for a seaman, invited me on the bridge. He was a young man, lean, fair, and morose, with lanky hair and a shuffling gait. As we left the miserable little wharf, he tossed his head contemptuously at the shore. 'Been living there?' he asked. I said, 'Yes.' 'Fine lot these government chaps—are they not?' he went on, speaking English with great precision and considerable bitterness. 'It is funny what some people will do for a few francs a month. I wonder what becomes of that kind when it goes upcountry?' I said to him I expected to see that soon. 'So-o-o!' he exclaimed. He shuffled athwart, keeping one eye ahead vigilantly. 'Don't be too sure,' he continued. 'The other day I took up a man who hanged himself on the road. He was a Swede, too.' 'Hanged himself! Why, in God's name?' I cried. He kept on looking out watchfully. 'Who knows? The sun too much for him, or the country perhaps.'

"At last we opened a reach. A rocky cliff appeared, mounds of turned-up earth by the shore, houses on a hill, others with iron roofs, amongst a waste of excavations, or hanging to the declivity. A continuous noise of the rapids above hovered over this scene of inhabited devastation. A lot of people, mostly black and naked, moved about like ants. A jetty projected into the river. A blinding sunlight drowned all this at times in a sudden recrudescence of glare. 'There's your Company's station,' said the Swede, pointing to three wooden barrack-like structures on the rocky slope. 'I will send your things up. Four boxes did you say? So. Farewell.'

"I came upon a boiler wallowing in the grass, then found a path leading up the hill. It turned aside for the boulders, and also for an undersized railway-truck lying there on its back with its wheels in the air. One was off. The thing looked as dead as the carcass of some animal. I came upon more pieces of decaying machinery, a stack of rusty rails. To the left a clump of trees made a shady spot, where dark things seemed to stir feebly. I blinked, the path was steep. A horn tooted to the right, and I saw the black people run. A heavy and dull detonation shook the ground, a puff of smoke came out of the cliff, and that was all. No change appeared on the face of the rock. They were building a railway. The cliff was not in the way or anything; but this objectless blasting was all the work going on.

"A slight clinking behind me made me turn my head. Six black men advanced in a file, toiling up the path. They walked erect and slow, balancing small baskets full of earth on their heads, and the clink kept time with their footsteps. Black rags were wound round their loins, and the short ends behind waggled to and fro like tails. I could see every rib, the joints of their limbs were like knots in a rope; each had an iron collar on his neck, and all were connected together with a chain whose bights swung between them, rhythmically clinking. Another report from the cliff made me think suddenly of that ship of war I had seen firing into a continent. It was the same kind of ominous voice; but these men could by no stretch of imagination be called enemies. They were called criminals, and the outraged law, like the bursting shells, had come to them, an insoluble mystery from the sea. All their meagre breasts panted together, the violently dilated nostrils quivered, the eyes stared stonily uphill. They passed me within six inches, without a glance, with that complete, deathlike indifference of unhappy savages. Behind this raw matter one of the reclaimed, the product of the new forces at work, strolled despondently, carrying a rifle by its middle. He had a uniform jacket with one button off, and seeing a white man on the path, hoisted his weapon to his shoulder with alacrity. This was simple prudence, white men being so much alike at a distance that he could not tell who I might be. He was speedily reassured, and with a large, white, rascally grin, and a glance at his charge, seemed to take me into partnership in his exalted trust. After all, I also was a part of the great cause of these high and just proceedings.

"Instead of going up, I turned and descended to the left. My idea was to let that chain-gang get out of sight before I climbed the hill. You know I am not particularly tender; I've had to strike and to fend off. I've had to resist and to attack sometimes—that's only one way of resisting—without counting the exact cost, according to the demands of such sort of life as I had blundered into. I've seen the devil of violence, and the devil of greed, and the devil of hot desire; but, by all the stars! these were strong, lusty, red-eyed devils, that swayed and drove men—men, I tell you. But as I stood on this hillside, I foresaw that in the blinding sunshine of that land I would become acquainted with a flabby, pretending, weak-eyed devil of a rapacious and pitiless folly. How insidious he could be, too, I was only to find out several months later and a thousand miles farther. For a moment I stood appalled, as though by a warning. Finally I descended the hill, obliquely, towards the trees I had seen.

"I avoided a vast artificial hole somebody had been digging on the slope, the purpose of which I found it impossible to divine. It wasn't a quarry or a sandpit, anyhow. It was just a hole. It might have been connected with the philanthropic desire of giving the criminals something to do. I don't know. Then I nearly fell into a very narrow ravine, almost no more than a scar in the hillside. I discovered that a lot of imported drainage-pipes for the settlement had been tumbled in there. There wasn't one that was not broken. It was a wanton smash-up. At last I got under the trees. My purpose was to stroll into the shade for a moment; but no sooner within than it seemed to me I had stepped into the gloomy circle of some Inferno. The rapids were near, and an uninterrupted, uniform, headlong, rushing noise filled the mournful stillness of the grove, where not a breath stirred, not a leaf moved, with a mysterious sound—as though the tearing pace of the launched earth had suddenly become audible.

"Black shapes crouched, lay, sat between the trees leaning against the trunks, clinging to the earth, half coming out, half effaced within the dim light, in all the attitudes of pain, abandonment, and despair. Another mine on the cliff went off, followed by a slight shudder of the soil under my feet. The work was going on. The work! And this was the place where some of the helpers had withdrawn to die.

"They were dying slowly—it was very clear. They were not enemies, they were not criminals, they were nothing earthly now—nothing but black shadows of disease and starvation, lying confusedly in the greenish gloom. Brought from all the recesses of the coast in all the legality of time contracts, lost in uncongenial surroundings, fed on unfamiliar food, they sickened, became inefficient, and were then allowed to crawl away and rest. These moribund shapes were free as air—and nearly as thin. I began to distinguish the gleam of the eyes under the trees. Then, glancing down, I saw a face near my hand. The black bones reclined at full length with one shoulder against the tree, and slowly the eyelids rose and the sunken eyes looked up at me, enormous and vacant, a kind of blind, white flicker in the depths of the orbs, which died out slowly. The man seemed young—almost a boy—but you know with them it's hard to tell. I found nothing else to do but to offer him one of my good Swede's ship's biscuits I had in my pocket. The fingers closed slowly on it and held—there was no other movement and no other glance. He had tied a bit of

white worsted round his neck—Why? Where did he
get it? Was it a badge—an ornament—a charm—a
propitiatory act? Was there any idea at all connected
with it? It looked startling round his black neck, this
bit of white thread from beyond the seas.

"Near the same tree two more bundles of acute
angles sat with their legs drawn up. One, with his chin
propped on his knees, started at nothing, in an intolerable and appalling manner: his brother phantom
rested its forehead, as if overcome with a great weari-
ness; and all about others were scattered in every pose
of contorted collapse, as in some picture of a massacre
or a pestilence. While I stood horror-struck, one of
these creatures rose to his hands and knees, and went
off on all-fours towards the river to drink. He lapped
out of his hand, then sat up in the sunlight, crossing
his shins in front of him, and after a time let his woolly
head fall on his breastbone.

"I didn't want any more loitering in the shade, and
I made haste towards the station. When near the
buildings I met a white man, in such an unexpected
elegance of get-up that in the first moment I took him
for a sort of vision. I saw a high starched collar, white
cuffs, a light alpaca jacket, snowy trousers, a clean
necktie, and varnished boots. No hat. Hair parted,
brushed, oiled, under a green-lined parasol held in a
big white hand. He was amazing, and had a penholder
behind his ear.

"I shook hands with this miracle, and I learned he
was the Company's chief accountant, and that all the
bookkeeping was done at this station. He had come
out for a moment, he said, 'to get a breath of fresh
air.' The expression sounded wonderfully odd, with
its suggestion of sedentary desk-life. I wouldn't have
mentioned the fellow to you at all, only it was from
his lips that I first heard the name of the man who is
so indissolubly connected with the memories of that
time. Moreover, I respected the fellow. Yes; I respected his collars, his vast cuffs, his brushed hair. His
appearance was certainly that of a hairdresser's
dummy; but in the great demoralization of the land he

kept up his appearance. That's backbone. His starched collars and got-up shirt-fronts were achievements of character. He had been out nearly three years; and, later, I could not help asking him how he managed to sport such linen. He had just the faintest blush, and said modestly, 'I've been teaching one of the native women about the station. It was difficult. She had a distaste for the work.' Thus this man had verily accomplished something. And he was devoted to his books, which were in apple-pie order.

"Everything else in the station was in a muddle— heads, things, buildings. Strings of dusty niggers with splay feet arrived and departed; a stream of manufactured goods, rubbishy cottons, beads, and brass-wire set into the depths of darkness, and in return came a precious trickle of ivory.

"I had to wait in the station for ten days—an eternity. I lived in a hut in the yard, but to be out of the chaos I would sometimes get into the accountant's office. It was built on horizontal planks, and so badly put together that, as he bent over his high desk, he was barred from neck to heels with narrow strips of sunlight. There was no need to open the big shutter to see. It was hot there, too; big flies buzzed fiendishly, and did not sting, but stabbed. I sat generally on the floor, while, of faultless appearance (and even slightly scented), perching on a high stool, he wrote, he wrote. Sometimes he stood up for exercise. When a truckle-bed with a sick man (some invalid agent from upcountry) was put in there, he exhibited a gentle annoyance. 'The groans of this sick person,' he said, 'distract my attention. And without that it is extremely difficult to guard against clerical errors in this climate.'

"One day he remarked, without lifting his head, 'In the interior you will no doubt meet Mr. Kurtz.' On my asking who Mr. Kurtz was, he said he was a first-class agent; and seeing my disappointment at this information, he added slowly, laying down his pen, 'He is a very remarkable person.' Further questions elicited from him that Mr. Kurtz was at present in charge of a trading-post, a very important one, in the true

ivory-country, at 'the very bottom of there. Sends in
as much ivory as all the other put together . . .' He
began to write again. The sick man was too ill to
groan. The flies buzzed in a great peace.

"Suddenly there was a growing murmur of voices
and a great tramping of feet. A caravan had come in.
A violent babble of uncouth sounds burst out on the
other side of the planks. All the carriers were speaking
together, and in the midst of the uproar the lamentable voice of the chief agent was heard 'giving it up'
tearfully for the twentieth time that day. . . . He rose
slowly. 'What a frightful row,' he said. He crossed the
room gently to look at the sick man, and returning,
said to me, 'He does not hear.' 'What! Dead?' I asked,
startled. 'No, not yet,' he answered, with great compo-
sure. Then, alluding with a toss of the head to the
tumult in the station-yard, 'When one has got to make
correct entries, one comes to hate those savages—hate
them to the death.' He remained thoughtful for a moment. 'When you see Mr. Kurtz' he went on, 'tell him
from me that everything here'—he glanced at the
deck—'is very satisfactory. I don't like to write to
him—with those messengers of ours you never know
who may get hold of your letter—at that Central Station.' He stared a me for a moment with his mild,
bulging eyes. 'Oh, he will go far, very far,' he began
again. 'He will be somebody in the Administration
before long. They, above—the Council of Europe, you
know—mean him to be.'

"He turned to his work. The noise outside had
ceased, and presently in going out I stopped at the
door. In the steady buzz of flies the homeward-bound
agent was lying flushed and insensible; the other, bent
over his books, was making correct entries of perfectly
correct transactions; and fifty feet below the doorstep
I could see the still tree-tops of the grove of death.

"Next day I left that station at last, with a caravan
of sixty men, for a two-hundred-mile tramp.

"No use telling you much about that. Paths, paths,
everywhere; a stamped-in network of paths spreading
over the empty land, through the long grass, through

burnt grass, through thickets, down and up chilly ra-
vines, up and down stony hills ablaze with heat; and
a solitude, a solitude, nobody, not a hut. The population had cleared out a long time ago. Well, if a lot
of mysterious niggers armed with all kinds of fearful
weapons suddenly took to travelling on the road between Deal and Gravesend, catching the yokels right
and left to carry heavy loads for them, I fancy every
farm and cottage thereabouts would get empty very
soon. Only here the dwellings were gone, too. Still
I passed through several abandoned villages. There's
something pathetically childish in the ruins of grass
walls. Day after day, with the stamp and shuffle of
sixty pair of bare feet behind me, each pair under a
60-lb. load. Camp, cook, sleep, strike camp, march.
Now and then a carrier dead in harness, at rest in the
long grass near the path, with an empty water-gourd
and his long staff lying by his side. A great silence
around and above. Perhaps on some quiet night the
tremor of far-off drums, sinking, swelling, a tremor
vast, faint; a sound weird, appealing, suggestive, and
wild—and perhaps with as profound a meaning as the
sound of bells in a Christian country. Once a white
man in an unbuttoned uniform, camping on the path
with an armed escort of lank Zanzibaris, very hospita-
ble and festive—not to say drunk. Was looking after
the upkeep of the road, he declared. Can't say I saw
any road or any upkeep, unless the body of a middle-
aged negro, with a bullet-hole in the forehead, upon
which I absolutely stumbled three miles farther on,
may be considered as a permanent improvement. I
had a white companion, too, not a bad chap, but
rather too fleshy and with the exasperating habit of
fainting on the hot hillsides, miles away from the least
bit of shade and water. Annoying, you know, to hold
your own coat like a parasol over a man's head while
he is coming to. I couldn't help asking him once what
he meant by coming there at all. 'To make money, of
course. What do you think?' he said, scornfully. Then
he got fever, and had to be carried in a hammock
slung under a pole. As he weighed sixteen stone I had

no end of rows with the carriers. They jibbed, ran away, sneaked off with their loads in the night—quite a mutiny. So, one evening, I made a speech in English with gestures, not one of which was lost to the sixty paris of eyes before me, and the next morning I started the hammock off in front all right. An hour afterwards I came upon the whole concern wrecked in a bush—man, hammock, groans, blankets, horrors. The heavy pole had skinned his poor nose. He was very anxious for me to kill somebody, but there wasn't the shadow of a carrier near. I remembered the old doctor—'It would be interesting for science to watch the mental changes of individuals, on the spot.' I felt I was becoming scientifically interesting. However, all that is to no purpose. On the fifteenth day I came in sight of the big river again, and hobbled into the Central Station. It was on a back water surrounded by scrub and forest, with a pretty border of smelly mud on one side, and on the three others enclosed by a crazy fence of rushes. A neglected gap was all the gate it had, and the first glance at the place was enough to let you see the flabby devil was running that show. White men with long staves in their hands appeared languidly from amongst the buildings, strolling up to take a look at me, and then retired out of sight somewhere. One of them, a stout, excitable chap with black moustaches, informed me with great volubility and many digressions, as soon as I told him who I was, that my steamer was at the bottom of the river. I was thunderstruck. What, how, why? Oh, it was 'all right.' The 'manager himself' was there. All quite correct. 'Everybody had behaved splendidly! splendidly!'— 'you must,' he said in agitation, 'go and see the general manager at once. He is waiting!'

"I did not see the real significance of that wreck at once. I fancy I see it now, but I am not sure—not at all. Certainly the affair was too stupid—when I think of it—to be altogether natural. Still . . . But at the moment it presented itself simply as a confounded nuisance. The steamer was sunk. They had started two days before in a sudden hurry up the river with the

manager on board, in charge of some volunteer skipper, and before they had been out three hours they
tore the bottom out of her on stones and she sank
near the south bank. I asked myself what I was to do
there, now my boat was lost. As a matter of fact, I
had plenty to do in fishing my command out of the
river. I had to set about it the very next day. That,
and the repairs when I brought the pieces to the station, took some months.

"My first interview with the manager was curious.
He did not ask me to sit down after my twenty-mile
walk that morning. He was commonplace in complexion, in feature, in manners, and in voice. He was of
middle size and of ordinary build. His eyes, of the
usual blue, were perhaps remarkably cold, and he certainly could make his glance fall on one as trenchant
and heavy as an axe. But even at these times the rest
of his person seemed to disclaim the intention. Otherwise there was only an indefinable, faint expression of
his lips, something stealthy—a smile—not a smile—I
remember it, but I can't explain. It was unconscious,
this smile was, though just after he had said something
it got intensified for an instant. It came at the end of
his speeches like a seal applied on the words to make
the meaning of the commonest phrase appear absolutely inscrutable. He was a common trader, from his
youth up employed in these parts—nothing more. He
was obeyed, yet he inspired neither love nor fear, nor
even respect. He inspired uneasiness. That was it! Uneasiness. Not a definite mistrust—just uneasiness—
nothing more. You have no idea how effective such
a . . . a . . . faculty can be. He had no genius for
organizing, for initiative, or for order even. That was
evident in such things as the deplorable state of the
station. He had no learning, and no intelligence. His
position had come to him—why? Perhaps because he
was never ill . . . He had served three terms of three
years out there . . . Because triumphant health in the
general rout of constitutions is a kind of power in
itself. When he went home on leave he rioted on a
large scale—pompously. Jack ashore—with a differ-

ence—in externals only. This one could gather from his casual talk. He originated nothing, he could keep the routine going—that's all. But he was great. He was great by this little thing that it was impossible to tell what could control such a man. He never gave that secret away. Perhaps there was nothing within him. Such a suspicion made one pause—for out there there were no external checks. Once when various tropical diseases had laid low almost every 'agent' in the station, he was heard to say, 'Men who come out here should have no entrails.' He sealed the utterance with that smile of his, as though it had been a door opening into a darkness he had in his keeping. You fancied you had seen things—but the seal was on. When annoyed at meal-times by the constant quarrels of the white men about precedence, he ordered an immense round table to be made, for which a special house had to be built. This was the station's mess-room. Where he sat was the first place—the rest were nowhere. One felt this to be his unalterable conviction. He was neither civil nor uncivil. He was quiet. He allowed his 'boy'—an overfed young negro from the coast—to treat the white men, under his very eyes, with provoking insolence.

"He began to speak as soon as he saw me. I had been very long on the road. He could not wait. Had to start without me. The up-river stations had to be relieved. There had been so many delays already that he did not know who was dead and who was alive, and how they got on—and so on, and so on. He paid no attention to my explanations, and, playing with a stick of sealing-wax, repeated several times that the situation was 'very grave, very grave.' There were rumours that a very important station was in jeopardy, and its chief, Mr. Kurtz, was ill. Hoped it was not true. Mr. Kurtz was . . . I felt weary and irritable. Hang Kurtz, I thought. I interrupted him by saying I had heard of Mr. Kurtz on the coast. 'Ah! So they talk of him down there,' he murmured to himself. Then he began again, assuring me Mr. Kurtz was the best agent he had, an exceptional man, of the greatest importance to the Company; therefore I could understand his anxiety. He was, he said, 'very, very uneasy.' Certainly he fidgeted on his chair a good deal, exclaimed, 'Ah, Mr. Kurtz!' broke the stick of sealing-wax and seemed dumfounded by accident. Next thing he wanted to know 'how long it would take to' . . , I interrupted him again. Being hungry, you know, and kept on my feet too, I was getting savage. 'How can I tell?' I said. 'I haven't even seen the wreck yet— some months, no doubt.' All this talk seemed to me so futile. 'Some months,' he said. 'Well, let us say three months before we can make a start. Yes. That ought to do the affair.' I flung out of his hut (he lived all alone in a clay hut with a sort of verandah) muttering to myself my opinion of him. He was a chattering idiot. Afterwards I took it back when it was borne in upon me startlingly with what extreme nicety he had estimated the time requisite for the 'affair.'

"I went to work the next day, turning, so to speak, my back on that station. In that way only it seemed to me I could keep my hold on the redeeming facts of life. Still, one must look about sometimes; and then I saw this station, these men strolling aimlessly about in the sunshine of the yard. I asked myself sometimes what it all meant. They wandered here and there with their absurd long staves in their hands, like a lot of faithless pilgrims bewitched inside a rotten fence. The word 'ivory' rang in the air, was whispered, was sighed. You would think they were praying to it. A taint of imbecile rapacity blew through it all, like a whiff from some corpse. By Jove! I've never seen anything so unreal in my life. And outside, the silent wilderness surrounding this cleared speck on the earth struck me as something great and invincible, like evil or truth, waiting patiently for the passing away of this fantastic invasion.

"Oh, these months! Well, never mind. Various things happened. One evening a grass shed full of calico, cotton prints, beads, and I don't know what else, burst into a blaze so suddenly that you would have thought the earth had opened to let an avenging fire consume all that trash. I was smoking my pipe quietly by my dismantled steamer, and saw them all cutting capers in the light, with their arms lifted high, when the stout man with moustaches came tearing down to the river, a tin pail in his hand, assured me that everybody was 'behaving splendidly, splendidly,' dipped about a quart of water and tore back again. I noticed there was a hole in the bottom of his pail.

"I strolled up. There was no hurry. You see the thing had gone off like a box of matches. It had been hopeless from the very first. The flame had leaped high, driven everybody back, lighted up everything—and collapsed. The shed was already a heap of embers glowing fiercely. A nigger was being beaten near by. They said he had caused the fire in some way; be that as it may, he was screeching most horribly. I saw him, later, for several days, sitting in a bit of shade looking very sick and trying to recover himself: afterwards he arose and went out—and the wilderness without a sound took him into its bosom again. As I approached the glow from the dark I found myself at the back of two men, talking. I heard the name of Kurtz pronounced, then the words, take advantage of his unfortunate accident.' One of the men was the manager. I wished him a good evening. 'Did you ever see anything like it—eh? it is incredible,' he said, and walked off. The other man remained. He was a first-class agent, young, gentlemanly, a bit reserved, with a forked little beard and a hooked nose. He was standoffish with the other agents, and they on their side said he was the manager's spy upon them. As to me, I had hardly ever spoken to him before. We got into talk, and by and by we strolled away from the hissing ruins. Then he asked me to his room, which was in the main building of the station. He struck a match, and I perceived that this young aristocrat had not only a silver-mounted dressing-case but also a whole candle all to himself. Just at that time the manager was the only man supposed to have any right to candles. Native mats covered the clay walls; a collection of spears, assegais, shields, knives was hung up in trophies. The business intrusted to this fellow was the making of bricks—so I had been informed; but there wasn't a fragment of a brick anywhere in the station, and he had been there more than a year—waiting. It seems he could not make bricks without something, I don't know what—straw maybe. Anyway, it could not be found there and as it was not likely to be sent from Europe, it did not appear clear to me what he was waiting for. An act of special creation perhaps. However, they were all waiting—all the sixteen or twenty pilgrims of them—for something; and upon my word it did not seem an uncongenial occupation, from the way they took it, though the only thing that ever came to them was disease—as far as I could see. They beguiled the time by back-biting and intriguing against each other in a foolish kind of way. There was an air of plotting about that station, but nothing came of it, of course. It was as unreal as everything else—as the philanthropic pretence of the whole concern, as their talk, as their government, as their show of work. The only real feeling was a desire to get appointed to a trading-post where ivory was to be had, so that they could earn percentages. They intrigued and slandered and hated each other only on that account—but as to effectually lifting a little finger—oh, no. By heavens! there is something after all in the world allowing one man to steal a horse while another must not look at a halter. Steal a horse straight out. Very well. He has done it. Perhaps he can ride. But there is a way of looking at a halter that would provoke the most charitable of saints into a kick.

"I had no idea why he wanted to be sociable, but as we chatted in there it suddenly occurred to me the fellow was trying to get at something—in fact, pumping me. He alluded constantly to Europe, to the people I was supposed to know there—putting leading questions as to my acquaintances in the sepulchral city, and so on. His little eyes glittered like mica discs—with curiosity—though he tried to keep up a bit of superciliousness. At first I was astonished, but very soon I became awfully curious to see what he

would find out from me. I couldn't possibly imagine
what I had in me to make it worth his while. It was
very pretty to see how he baffled himself, for in truth
my body was full only of chills, and my head had
nothing in it but that wretched steamboat business.
It was evident he took me for a perfectly shameless
prevaricator. At last he got angry, and, to conceal a
movement of furious annoyance, he yawned. I rose.
Then I noticed a small sketch of oils, on a panel, rep-
resenting a woman, draped and blindfolded, carrying
a lighted torch. The background was sombre—almost
black. The movement of the woman was stately, and
the effect of the torchlight on the face was sinister.

"It arrested me, and he stood by civilly, holding an
empty half-pint champagne bottle (medical comforts)
with the candle stuck in it. To my question he said
Mr. Kurtz had painted this—in this very station more
than a year ago—while waiting for means to go to
his trading-post. 'Tell me, pray,' said I, 'who is this
Mr. Kurtz?'

" 'The chief of the Inner Station,' he answered in a
short tone, looking away. 'Much obliged,' I said,
laughing. 'And you are the brickmaker of the Central
Station. Every one knows that.' He was silent for a
while. 'He is a prodigy,' he said at last. 'He is an
emissary of pity and science and progress, and devil
knows what else. We want,' he began to declaim suddenly, 'for the guidance of the cause intrusted to us
by Europe, so to speak, higher intelligence, wide sym-
pathies, a singleness of purpose.' 'Who says that?' I
asked. 'Lots of them,' he replied. 'Some even write
that; and so *he* comes here, a special being, as you
ought to know.' 'Why ought I to know?' I interrupted,
really surprised. He paid no attention. 'Yes. Today he
is chief of the best station, next year he will be assistant-manager, two years more and . . . but I daresay
you know what he will be in two years' time. You are
of the new gang—the gang of virtue. The same people
who sent him specially also recommended you. Oh,
don't say so. I've my own eyes to trust.' Light dawned
upon me. My dear aunt's influential acquaintances

were producing an unexpected effect upon that young man. I nearly burst into a laugh. 'Do you read the Company's confidential correspondence?' I asked. He hadn't a word to say. It was great fun. 'When Mr. Kurtz,' I continued, severely, 'is General Manager, you won't have the opportunity.'

"He blew the candle out suddenly, and we went outside. The moon had risen. Black figures strolled about listlessly, pouring water on the glow, whence proceeded a sound of hissing; steam ascended in the moonlight, the beaten nigger groaned somewhere. 'What a row the brute makes!' said the indefatigable man with the moustaches, appearing near us. 'Serve him right. Transgression—punishment—bang! Pitiless, pitiless. That's the only way. This will prevent all con-flagrations for the future. I was just telling the manager . . .' He noticed my companion, and became crestfallen all at once. 'Not in bed yet,' he said, with a kind of servile heartiness; 'it's so natural. Ha! Dan-ger—agitation.' He vanished. I went on to the river-side, and the other followed me. I heard a scathing murmur at my ear. 'Heap of muffs—go to.' The pil-grims could be seen in knots gesticulating, discussing. Several had still their staves in their hands. I verily believe they took these sticks to bed with them. Be-yond the fence the forest stood up spectrally in the moonlight, and through the dim stir, through the faint sounds of that lamentable courtyard, the silence of the land went home to one's very heart—its mystery, its greatness, the amazing reality of its concealed life. The hurt nigger moaned feebly somewhere near by, and then fetched a deep sigh that made me mend my pace away from there. I felt a hand introducing itself under my arm. 'My dear sir,' said the fellow, 'I don't want to be misunderstood, and especially by you, who will see Mr. Kurtz long before I can have that pleasure. I wouldn't like him to get a false idea of my disposition. . . .'

"I let him run on, this papier-maché Mephisto-pheles, and it seemed to me that if I tried I could poke my forefinger through him, and would find noth-

ing inside but a little loose dirt, maybe. He, don't you
see, had been planning to be assistant-manager by and
by under the present man, and I could see that the
coming of that Kurtz had upset them both not a little.
He talked precipitately, and I did not try to stop him.
I had my shoulders against the wreck of my steamer,
hauled up on the slope like a carcass of some big river
animal. The smell of mud, of primeval mud, by Jove!
was in my nostrils, the high stillness of primeval forest
was before my eyes; there were shiny patches on the
black creek. The moon had spread over everything a
thin layer of silver—over the rank grass, over the mud,
upon the wall of matted vegetation standing higher
than the wall of a temple, over the great river I could
see through a sombre gap glittering, glittering, as it
flowed broadly by without a murmur. All this was
great, expectant, mute, while the man jabbered about
himself. I wondered whether the stillness on the face
of the immensity looking at us two were meant as an
appeal or as a menace. What were we who had stayed
in here? Could we handle that dumb thing, or would
it handle us? I felt how big, how confoundedly big,
was that thing that couldn't talk, and perhaps was deaf
as well. What was in there? I could see a little ivory
coming out from there, and I had heard Mr. Kurtz
was in there. I had heard enough about it, too—God
knows! Yet somehow it didn't bring any image with
it—no more than if I had been told an angel or a
fiend was in there. I believed it in the same way one
of you might believe there are inhabitants in the
planet Mars. I knew once a Scotch sailmaker who was
certain, dead sure, there were people in Mars. If you
asked him for some idea how they looked and behaved, he would get shy and mutter something about
'walking on all-fours.' If you as much as smiled, he
would—though a man of sixty—offer to fight you. I
would not have gone so far as to fight for Kurtz, but
I went for him near enough to a lie. You know I hate,
detest, and can't bear a lie, not because I am straighter
than the rest of us, but simply because it appalls me.
There is a taint of death, a flavour of mortality in

lies—which is exactly what I hate and detest of the world—what I want to forget. It makes me miserable and sick, like biting something rotten would do. Temperament, I suppose. Well, I went near enough to it by letting the young fool there believe anything he liked to imagine as to my influence in Europe. I became in an instant as much of a pretence as the rest of the bewitched pilgrims. This simply because I had a notion it somehow would be of help to that Kurtz whom at the time I did not see—you understand. He was just a word for me. I did not see the man in the name any more than you do. Do you see him? Do you see the story? Do you see anything? It seems to me I am trying to tell you a dream—making a vain attempt, because no relation of a dream can convey the dream-sensation, that commingling of absurdity, surprise, and bewilderment in a tremor of struggling revolt, that notion of being captured by the incredible which is of the very essence of dreams. . . ."

He was silent for a while.

". . . No, it is impossible; it is impossible to convey the life-sensation of any given epoch of one's existence—that which makes its truth, its meaning—its subtle and penetrating essence. It is impossible. We live, as we dream—alone. . . ."

He paused again as if reflecting, then added:

"Of course in this you fellows see more than I could then. You see me, whom you know. . . ."

It had become so pitch dark that we listeners could hardly see one another. For a long time already he, sitting apart, had been no more to us than a voice. There was not a word from anybody. The others might have been asleep, but I was awake. I listened, I listened on the watch for the sentence, for the word, that would give me the clue to the faint uneasiness inspired by this narrative that seemed to shape itself without human lips in the heavy night-air of the river.

". . . Yes—I let him run on," Marlow began again, "and think what he pleased about the powers that were behind me. I did! And there was nothing behind me! There was nothing but that wretched, old, man-

gled steamboat I was leaning against, while he talked
fluently about 'the necessity for every man to get on.'
'And when one comes out here, you conceive, it is
not to gaze at the moon.' Mr. Kurtz was a 'universal
genius,' but even a genius would find it easier to work
with 'adequate tools—intelligent men.' He did not
make bricks—why, there was a physical impossibility
in the way—as I was well aware; and if he did secretarial work for the manager, it was because 'no sensible man rejects wantonly the confidence of his
superiors.' Did I see it? I saw it. What more did I
want? What I really wanted was rivets, by heaven!
Rivets. To get on with the work—to stop the hole.
Rivets I wanted. There were cases of them down at
the coast—cases—piled up—burst—split! You kicked
a loose rivet at every second step in that station-yard
on the hillside. Rivets had rolled into the grove of
death. You could fill your pockets with rivets for the
trouble of stooping down—and there wasn't one rivet
to be found where it was wanted. We had plates that
would do, but nothing to fasten them with. And every
week the messenger, a lone negro, letter-bag on shoulder and staff in hand, left our station for the coast.
And several times a week a coast caravan came in
with trade goods—ghastly glazed calico that made you
shudder only to look at it, glass beads value about a
penny a quart, confounded spotted cotton handker-
chiefs. And no rivets. Three carriers could have
brought all that was wanted to set that steamboat
afloat.

"He was becoming confidential now, but I fancy my
unresponsive attitude must have exasperated him at
last, for he judged it necessary to inform me he feared
neither God nor devil, let alone any mere man. I said
I could see that very well, but what I wanted was a
certain quantity of rivets—and rivets were what really
Mr. Kurtz wanted, if he had only known it. Now letters went to the coast every week. . . . 'My dear sir,'
he cried, 'I write from dictation.' I demanded rivets.
There was a way—for an intelligent man. He changed
his manner; became very cold, and suddenly began to

talk about a hippopotamus; wondered whether sleeping on board the steamer (I stuck to my salvage night
and day) I wasn't disturbed. There was an old hippo
that had the bad habit of getting out on the bank and
roaming at night over the station grounds. The pilgrims used to turn out in a body and empty every rifle
they could lay hands on at him. Some even had sat
up o' nights for him. All this energy was wasted,
though. 'That animal has a charmed life,' he said; 'but
you can say this only of brutes in this country. No
man—you apprehend me?—no man here bears a
charmed life.' He stood there for a moment in the
moonlight with his delicate hooked nose set a little
askew, and his mica eyes glittering without a wink,
then, with a curt Good-night, he strode off. I could
see he was disturbed and considerably puzzled, which
made me feel more hopeful than I had been for days.
It was a great comfort to turn from that chap to my
influential friend, the battered, twisted, ruined, tin-pot
steamboat. I clambered on board. She rang under my
feet like an empty Huntley & Palmer biscuit-tin
kicked along a gutter; she was nothing so solid in
make, and rather less pretty in shape, but I had ex-
pended enough hard work on her to make me love
her. No influential friend would have served me better. She had given me a chance to come out a bit—
to find out what I could do. No, I don't like work. I
had rather laze about and think of all the fine things
that can be done. I don't like work—no man does—
but I like what is in the work—the chance to find
yourself. Your own reality—for yourself, not for others—what no other man can ever know. They can only
see the mere show, and never can tell what it really
means.

"I was not surprised to see somebody sitting aft, on
the deck, with his legs dangling over the mud. You
see I rather chummed with the few mechanics there
were in that station, whom the other pilgrims naturally
despised—on account of their imperfect manners, I
suppose. This was the foreman—a boiler-maker by
trade—a good worker. He was a lank, bony, yellow-

faced man, with big intense eyes. His aspect was worried, and his head was as bald as the palm of my hand;
but his hair in falling seemed to have stuck to his chin,
and had prospered in the new locality, for his beard
hung down to his waist. He was a widower with six
young children (he had left them in charge of a sister
of his to come out there), and the passion of his life
was pigeon-flying. He was an enthusiast and a connois-
seur. He would rave about pigeons. After work hours
he used sometimes to come over from his hut for a
talk about his children and his pigeons; at work, when
he had to crawl in the mud under the bottom of the
steamboat, he would tie up that beard of his in a kind
of white serviette he brought for the purpose. It had
loops to go over his ears. In the evening he could be
seen squatted on the bank rinsing that wrapper in the
creek with great care, then spreading it solemnly on
a bush to dry.

"I slapped him on the back and shouted, 'We shall
have rivets!' He scrambled to his feet exclaiming, 'No!
Rivets!' as though he couldn't believe his ears. Then
in a low voice, 'You . . . eh?' I don't know why we
behaved like lunatics. I put my finger to the side of
my nose and nodded mysteriously. 'Good for you!' he
cried, snapped his fingers above his head, lifting one
foot. I tried a jig. We capered on the iron deck. A
frightful clatter came out of that hulk, and the virgin
forest on the other bank of the creek sent it back in
a thundering roll upon the sleeping station. It must
have made some of the pilgrims sit up in their hovels.
A dark figure obscured the lighted doorway of the
manager's hut, vanished, then, a second or so after,
the doorway itself vanished, too. We stopped, and the
silence driven away by the stamping of our feet flowed
back again from the recesses of the land. The great
wall of vegetation, an exuberant and entangled mass
of trunks, branches, leaves, boughs, festoons, motionless in the moonlight, was like a rioting invasion
of soundless life, a rolling wave of plants, piled up,
crested, ready to topple over the creek, to sweep every
little man of us out of his little existence. And it

moved not. A deadened burst of mighty splashes and snorts reached us from afar, as though an ichthyosaurus had been taking a bath of glitter in the great river. 'After all,' said the boiler-maker in a reasonable tone, 'why shouldn't we get the rivets?' Why not, indeed! I did not know of any reason why we shouldn't. 'They'll come in three weeks,' I said confidently.

"But they didn't. Instead of rivets there came an invasion, an infliction, a visitation. It came in sections during the next three weeks, each section headed by a donkey carrying a white man in new clothes and tan shoes, bowing from that elevation right and left to the impressed pilgrims. A quarrelsome band of footsore sulky niggers trod on the heels of the donkey; a lot of tents, campstools, tin boxes, white cases, brown bales would be shot down in the court-yard, and the air of mystery would deepen a little over the muddle of the station. Five such instalments came, with their absurd air of disorderly flight with the loot of innumerable outfit shops and provision stores, that, one would think, they were lugging, after a raid, into the wilderness for equitable division. It was an inextricable mess of things decent in themselves but that human folly made look like the spoils of thieving.

"This devoted band called itself the Eldorado Exploring Expedition, and I believe they were sworn to secrecy. Their talk, however, was the talk of sordid buccaneers: it was reckless without hardihood, greedy without audacity, and cruel without courage; there was not an atom of foresight or of serious intention in the whole batch of them, and they did not seem aware these things are wanted for the work of the world. To tear treasure out of the bowels of the land was their desire, with no more moral purpose at the back of it than there is in burglars breaking into a safe. Who paid the expenses of the noble enterprise I don't know; but the uncle of our manager was leader of that lot.

"In exterior he resembled a butcher in a poor neighbourhood, and his eyes had a look of sleepy cunning. He carried his fat paunch with ostentation on his short legs, and during the time his gang infested the station spoke to no one but his nephew. You could see these two roaming about all day long with their heads close together in an everlasting confab.

"I had given up worrying myself about the rivets. One's capacity for that kind of folly is more limited than you would suppose. I said Hang!—and let things slide. I would give some thought to Kurtz. I wasn't very interested in him. No. Still, I was curious to see whether this man, who had come out equipped with moral ideas of some sort, would climb to the top after all and how he would set about his work when there."

II

"One evening as I was lying flat on the deck of my steamboat, I heard voices approaching—and there were the nephew and the uncle strolling along the bank. I laid my head on my arm again, and had nearly lost myself in a doze, when somebody said in my ear, as it were: 'I am as harmless as a little child, but I don't like to be dictated to. Am I the manager—or am I not? I was ordered to send him there. It's incredible.'. . . I became aware that the two were standing on the shore alongside the forepart of the steamboat, just below my head. I did not move; it did not occur to me to move: I was sleepy. 'It *is* unpleasant,' grunted the uncle. 'He has asked the Administration to be sent there,' said the other, 'with the idea of showing what he could do; and I was instructed accordingly. Look at the influence that man must have. Is it not frightful?' They both agreed it was frightful, then made several bizarre remarks: 'Make rain and fine weather—one man—the Council—by the nose'—bits of absurd sentences that got the better of my drowsiness, so that I had pretty near the whole of my wits about me when the uncle said, 'The climate may do away with this difficulty for you. Is he alone there?' 'Yes,' answered the manager; 'he sent his assistant down the river with a note to me in these terms:

"Clear this poor devil out of the country, and don't bother sending more of that sort. I had rather be alone than have the kind of men you can dispose of with me." It was more than a year ago. Can you imagine such impudence!' 'Anything since then?' asked the other hoarsely. 'Ivory,' jerked the nephew; 'lots of it—prime sort—lots—most annoying, from him.' 'And with that?' questioned the heavy rumble. 'Invoice,' was the reply fired out, so to speak. Then silence. They had been talking about Kurtz.

"I was broad awake by this time, but, lying perfectly at ease, remained still, having no inducement to change my position. 'How did that ivory come all this way?' growled the elder man, who seemed very vexed. The other explained that it had come with a fleet of canoes in charge of an English half-caste clerk Kurtz had with him; that Kurtz had apparently intended to return himself, the station being by that time bare of goods and stores, but after coming three hundred miles, had suddenly decided to go back, which he started to do alone in a small dugout with four paddlers, leaving the half-caste to continue down the river with the ivory. The two fellows there seemed astounded at anybody attempting such a thing. They were at a loss for an adequate motive. As to me, I seemed to see Kurtz for the first time. It was a distant glimpse: the dugout, four paddling savages, and the lone white man turning his back suddenly on the head-quarters, on relief, on thoughts of home—perhaps; setting his face towards the depths of the wilderness, towards his empty and desolate station. I did not know the motive. Perhaps he was just simply a fine fellow who stuck to his work for its own sake. His name, you understand, had not been pronounced once. He was 'that man.' The half-caste, who, as far as I could see, had conducted a difficult trip with great prudence and pluck, was invariably alluded to as 'that scoundrel.' The 'scoundrel' had recovered imperfectly. . . . The two below me moved away then a few paces, and strolled back and forth at some little distance. I heard: 'Military post—doctor—two hundred miles—quite alone now—unavoidable delays—nine months—no news—strange rumours.' They approached again, just as the manager was saying, 'No one, as far as I know, unless a species of wandering trader—a pestilential fellow, snapping ivory from the natives.' Who was it they were talking about now? I gathered in snatches that this was some man supposed to be in Kurtz's district, and of whom the manager did not approve. 'We will not be free from unfair competition till one of these fellows is hanged for an example,' he said. 'Certainly,' grunted the other; 'get him hanged! Why not? Anything—anything can be done in this country. That's what I say; nobody here, you understand, *here*, can endanger your position. And why? You stand the climate—you outlast them all. The danger is in Europe; but there before I left I took care to——' They moved off and whispered, then their voices rose again. 'The extraordinary series of delays is not my fault. I did my best.' The fat man sighed. 'Very sad.' 'And the pestiferous absurdity of his talk,' continued the other; 'he bothered me enough when he was here. "Each station should be like a beacon on the road towards better things, a centre for trade of course, but also for humanizing, improving, instructing." Conceive you—that ass! And he wants to be manager! No, it's——' Here he got choked by excessive indignation, and I lifted my head the least bit. I was surprised to see how near they were—right under me. I could have spat upon their hats. They were looking on the ground, absorbed in thought. The manager was switching his leg with a slender twig: his sagacious relative lifted his head. 'You have been well since you came out this time?' he asked. The other gave a start. 'Who? I? Oh! Like a charm—like a charm. But the rest—oh, my goodness! All sick. They die so quick, too, that I haven't the time to send them out of the country—it's incredible!' 'H'm. Just so,' grunted the uncle. 'Ah! my body, trust to this—I say, trust to this.' I saw him extend his short flipper of an arm for a gesture that took in the forest, the creek, the mud, the river—seemed to beckon with a dishonouring flourish before the sunlit

face of the land a treacherous appeal to the lurking
death, to the hidden evil, to the profound darkness of
its heart. It was so startling that I leaped to my feet
and looked back at the edge of the forest, as though
I had expected an answer of some sort to that black
display of confidence. You know the foolish notions
that come to one sometimes. The high stillness confronted these two figures with its ominous patience,
waiting for the passing away of a fantastic invasion.

"They swore aloud together—out of sheer fright, I
believe—then pretending not to know anything of my
existence, turned back to the station. The sun was low;
and leaning forward side by side, they seemed to be
tugging painfully uphill their two ridiculous shadows
of unequal length, that trailed behind them slowly
over the tall grass without bending a single blade.

"In a few days the Eldorado Expedition went into
the patient wilderness, that closed upon it as the sea
closes over a diver. Long afterwards the news came
that all the donkeys were dead. I know nothing as to
the fate of the less valuable animals. They, no doubt,
like the rest of us, found what they deserved. I did
not inquire. I was then rather excited at the prospect
of meeting Kurtz very soon. When I say very soon I
mean it comparatively. It was just two months from
the day we left the creek when we came to the bank
below Kurtz's station.

"Going up that river was like travelling back to the
earliest beginnings of the world, when vegetation rioted on the earth and the big trees were kings. An
empty stream, a great silence, an impenetrable forest.
The air was warm, thick, heavy, sluggish. There was
no joy in the brilliance of sunshine. The long stretches
of the waterway ran on, deserted, into the gloom of
over-shadowed distances. On silvery sand-banks
hippos and alligators sunned themselves side by side.
The broadening waters flowed through a mob of
wooded islands; you lost your way on that river as you
would in a desert, and butted all day long against
shoals, trying to find the channel, till you thought
yourself bewitched and cut off for ever from every-

thing you had known once—somewhere—far away—
in another existence perhaps. There were moments
when one's past came back to one, as it will sometimes
when you have not a moment to spare to yourself;
but it came in the shape of an unrestful and noisy
dream, remembered with wonder amongst the overwhelming realities of this strange world of plants, and
water, and silence. And this stillness of life did not in
the least resemble a peace. It was the stillness of an
implacable force brooding over an inscrutable intention. It looked at you with a vengeful aspect. I got
used to it afterwards; I did not see it any more; I had
no time. I had to keep guessing at the channel; I had
to discern, mostly by inspiration, the signs of hidden
banks; I watched for sunken stones; I was leaning to
clap my teeth smartly before my heart flew out, when
I shaved by a fluke some infernal sly old snag that
would have ripped the life out of the tin-pot steamboat and drowned all the pilgrims; I had to keep a
lookout for the signs of dead wood we could cut up
in the night for next day's steaming. When you have
to attend to things of that sort, to the mere incidents
of the surface, the reality—the reality, I tell you—
fades. The inner truth is hidden—luckily, luckily. But
I felt it all the same; I felt often its mysterious stillness
watching me at my monkey tricks, just as it watches
you fellows performing on your respective tight-ropes
for—what is it? half-a-crown a tumble——"

"Try to be civil, Marlow," growled a voice, and I
knew there was at least one listener awake besides
myself.

"I beg your pardon. I forgot the heartache which
makes up the rest of the price. And indeed what does
the price matter, if the trick be well done? You do
your tricks very well. And I didn't do badly either,
since I managed not to sink that steamboat on my first
trip. It's a wonder to me yet. Imagine a blindfolded
man set to drive a van over a bad road. I sweated and
shivered over that business considerably, I can tell
you. After all, for a seaman, to scrape the bottom of
the thing that's supposed to float all the time under

his care is the unpardonable sin. No one may know
of it, but you never forget the thump—eh? A blow on
the very heart. You remember it, you dream of it, you
wake up at night and think of it—years after—and go
hot and cold all over. I don't pretend to say that
steamboat floated all the time. More than once she
had to wade for a bit, with twenty cannibals splashing
around and pushing. We had enlisted some of these
chaps on the way for a crew. Fine fellows—cannibals—in their place. They were men one could work
with, and I am grateful to them. And, after all, they
did not eat each other before my face: they had
brought along a provision of hippo-meat which went
rotten, and made the mystery of the wilderness stink
in my nostrils. Phoo! I can sniff it now. I had the
manager on board and three or four pilgrims with
their staves—all complete. Sometimes we came upon
a station close by the bank, clinging to the skirts of
the unknown, and the white men rushing out of a
tumble-down hovel, with great gestures of joy and surprise and welcome, seemed very strange—had the appearance of being held there captive by a spell. The
word ivory would ring in the air for a while—and on
we went again into the silence, along empty reaches,
round the still bends, between the high walls of our
winding way, reverberating in hollow claps the ponderous beat of the stern-wheel. Trees, trees, millions
of trees, massive, immense, running up high; and at
their foot, hugging the bank against the stream, crept
the little begrimed steamboat, like a sluggish beetle
crawling on the floor of a lofty portico. It made you
feel very small, very lost, and yet it was not altogether
depressing, that feeling. After all, if you were small,
the grimy beetle crawled on—which was just what you
wanted it to do. Where the pilgrims imagined it
crawled to I don't know. To some place where they
expected to get something. I bet! For me it crawled
towards Kurtz—exclusively; but when the steam-pipes
started leaking we crawled very slow. The reaches
opened before us and closed behind, as if the forest
had stepped leisurely across the water to bar the way

for our return. We penetrated deeper and deeper into
the heart of darkness. It was very quiet there. At night
sometimes the roll of drums behind the curtain of
trees would run up the river and remain sustained
faintly, as if hovering in the air high over our heads,
till the first break of day. Whether it meant war, peace,
or prayer we could not tell. The dawns were heralded
by the descent of a chill stillness; the wood-cutters
slept, their fires burned low; the snapping of a twig
would make you start. We were wanderers on a prehistoric earth, on an earth that wore the aspect of an
unknown planet. We could have fancied ourselves the
first of men taking possession of an accursed inheri-
tance, to be subdued at the cost of profound anguish
and of excessive toil. But suddenly, as we struggled
round a bend, there would be a glimpse of rush walls,
of peaked grass-roofs, a burst of yells, a whirl of black
limbs, a mass of hands clapping, of feet stamping, of
bodies swaying, of eyes rolling, under the droop of
heavy and motionless foliage. The steamer toiled
along slowly on the edge of a black and incomprehensible frenzy. The prehistoric man was cursing us, praying to us, welcoming us—who could tell? We were cut
off from the comprehension of our surroundings; we
glided past like phantoms, wondering and secretly appalled, as sane men would be before an enthusiastic
outbreak in a madhouse. We could not understand
because we were too far and could not remember because we were travelling in the night of first ages, of
those ages that are gone, leaving hardly a sign—and
no memories.

"The earth seemed unearthly. We are accustomed to
look upon the shackled form of a conquered monster,
but there—there you could look at a thing monstrous
and free. It was unearthly, and the men were—— No,
they were not inhuman. Well, you know, that was the
worst of it—this suspicion of their not being inhuman.
It would come slowly to one. They howled and leaped,
and spun, and made horrid faces; but what thrilled
you was just the thought of their humanity—like
yours—the thought of your remote kinship with this

wild and passionate uproar. Ugly. Yes, it was ugly
enough; but if you were man enough you would admit
to yourself that there was in you just the faintest trace
of a response to the terrible frankness of that noise,
a dim suspicion of there being a meaning in it which
you—you so remote from the night of first ages—
could comprehend. And why not? The mind of man
is capable of anything—because everything is in it, all
the past as well as all the future. What was there after
all? Joy, fear, sorrow, devotion, valour, rage—who can
tell?—but truth—truth stripped of its cloak of time.
Let the fool gape and shudder—the man knows, and
can look on without a wink. But he must at least be
as much of a man as these on the shore. He must
meet the truth with his own true stuff—with his own
inborn strength. Principles won't do. Acquisitions,
clothes, pretty rags—rags that would fly off at the first
good shake. No; you want a deliberate belief. An appeal to me in this fiendish row—is there? Very well;
I hear; I admit, but I have a voice, too, and for good
or evil mine is the speech that cannot be silenced. Of
course, a fool, what with sheer fright and fine sentiments, is always safe. Who's that grunting? You wonder I didn't go ashore for a howl and a dance? Well,
no—I didn't. Fine sentiments, you say? Fine sentiments, be hanged! I had no time. I had to mess about
with white-lead and strips of woolen blanket helping
to put bandages on those leaky steampipes—I tell you.
I had to watch the steering, and circumvent those
snags, and get the tin-pot along by hook or by crook.
There was surface-truth enough in these things to save
a wiser man. And between whiles I had to look after
the savage who was fireman. He was an improved
specimen; he could fire up a vertical boiler. He was
there below me, and, upon my word, to look at him
was as edifying as seeing a dog in a parody of breeches
and a feather hat, walking on his hind-legs. A few
months of training had done for that really fine chap.
He squinted at the steam-gauge and at the water-
gauge with an evident effort of intrepidity—and he
had filed teeth, too, the poor devil, and the wool of

his pate shaved into queer patterns, and three ornamental scars on each of his cheeks. He ought to have
been clapping his hands and stamping his feet on the
bank, instead of which he was hard at work, a thrall
of strange witchcraft, full of improving knowledge. He
was useful because he had been instructed; and what
he knew was this—that should the water in that trans-
parent thing disappear, the evil spirit inside the boiler
would get angry through the greatness of his thirst,
and take a terrible vengeance. So he sweated and fired
up and watched the glass fearfully (with an impromptu
charm, made of rags, tied to his arm, and a piece of
polished bone, as big as a watch, stuck flatways
through his lower lip), while the wooded banks slipped
past us slowly, the short noise was left behind, the
interminable miles of silence—and we crept on, towards Kurtz. But the snags were thick, the water was
treacherous and shallow, the boiler seemed indeed to
have a sulky devil in it, and thus neither that fireman
nor I had any time to peer into our creepy thoughts.

"Some fifty miles below the Inner Station we came
upon a hut of reeds, an inclined and melancholy pole,
with the unrecognizable tatters of what had been a
flag of some sort flying from it, and a neatly stacked
wood-pile. This was unexpected. We came to the
bank, and on the stack of firewood found a flat piece
of board with some faded pencil-writing on it. When
deciphered it said: 'Wood for you. Hurry up. Approach cautiously.' There was a signature, but it was
illegible—not Kurtz—a much longer word. 'Hurry up.'
Where? Up the river? 'Approach cautiously.' We had
not done so. But the warning could not have been
meant for the place where it could be only found after
approach. Something was wrong above. But what—
and how much? That was the question. We com-
mented adversely upon the imbecility of that tele-
graphic style. The bush around said nothing, and
would not let us look very far, either. A torn curtain
of red twill hung in the doorway of the hut, and
flapped sadly in our faces. The dwelling was dismantled; but we could see a white man had lived there

not very long ago. There remained a rude table—a
plank of two posts; a heap of rubbish reposed in a
dark corner, and by the door I picked up a book. It
had lost its covers, and the pages had been thumbed
into a state of extremely dirty softness; but the back
had been lovingly stitched afresh with white cotton
thread, which looked clean yet. It was an extraordinary find. Its title was, *An Inquiry into some Points of
Seamanship,* by a man Towser, Towson—some such
name—Master in his Majesty's Navy. The matter
looked dreary reading enough, with illustrative dia-
grams and repulsive tables of figures, and the copy
was sixty years old. I handled this amazing antiquity
with the greatest possible tenderness, lest it should
dissolve in my hands. Within, Towson or Towser was
inquiring earnestly into the breaking strain of ships'
chains and tackles, and other such matters. Not a very
enthralling book; but at the first glance you could see
there a singleness of intention, an honest concern for
the right way of going to work, which made these
humble pages, thought out so many years ago, luminous with another than a professional light. The simple old sailor, with his talk of chains and purchases,
made me forget the jungle and the pilgrims in a deli-
cious sensation of having come upon something un-
mistakably real. Such a book being there was
wonderful enough; but still more astounding were the
notes pencilled in the margin, and plainly referring to
the text. I couldn't believe my eyes! They were in
cipher! Yes, it looked like cipher. Fancy a man lugging
with him a book of that description into this nowhere
and studying it—and making notes—in cipher at that!
It was an extravagant mystery.

"I had been dimly aware for some time of a worrying noise, and when I lifted my eyes I saw the wood-
pile was gone, and the manager, aided by all the pilgrims, was shouting at me from the riverside. I slipped
the book into my pocket. I assure you to leave off
reading was like tearing myself away from the shelter
of an old and solid friendship.

"I started the lame engine ahead. 'It must be this

miserable trader—this intruder,' exclaimed the manager, looking back malevolently at the place we had
left. 'He must be English,' I said. 'It will not save him
from getting into trouble if he is not careful,' muttered
the manager darkly. I observed with assumed inno-
cence that no man was safe from trouble in this world.

"The current was more rapid now, the steamer
seemed at her last gasp, the stern-wheel flopped languidly, and I caught myself listening on tiptoe for the
next beat of the boat, for in sober truth I expected
the wretched thing to give up every moment. It was
like watching the last flickers of a life. But still we
crawled. Sometimes I would pick out a tree a little
way ahead to measure our progress towards Kurtz by,
but I lost it invariably before we got abreast. To keep
the eyes so long on one thing was too much for human
patience. The manager displayed a beautiful resigna-
tion. I fretted and fumed and took to arguing with
myself whether or no I would talk openly with Kurtz;
but before I could come to any conclusion it occurred
to me that my speech or my silence, indeed any action
of mine, would be a mere futility. What did it matter
what any one knew or ignored? What did it matter
who was manager? One gets sometimes such a flash
of insight. The essentials of this affair lay deep under
the surface, beyond my reach, and beyond my power
of meddling.

"Towards the evening of the second day we judged
ourselves about eight miles from Kurtz's station. I
wanted to push on; but the manager looked grave,
and told me the navigation up there was so dangerous
that it would be advisable, the sun being very low
already, to wait where we were till next morning.
Moreover, he pointed out that if the warning to approach cautiously were to be followed, we must approach in daylight—not at dusk or in the dark. This
was sensible enough. Eight miles meant nearly three
hours' steaming for us, and I could also see suspicious
ripples at the upper end of the reach. Nevertheless, I
was annoyed beyond expression at the delay, and most
unreasonably, too, since one night more could not

matter much after so many months. As we had plenty
of wood, and caution was the word, I brought up in
the middle of the stream. The reach was narrow,
straight, with high sides like a railway cutting. The
dusk came gliding into it long before the sun had set.
The current ran smooth and swift, but a dumb immo
bility sat on the banks. The living trees, lashed together by the creepers and every living bush of the
undergrowth, might have been changed into stone,
even to the slenderest twig, to the lightest leaf. It was
not sleep—it seemed unnatural, like a state of trance.
Not the faintest sound of any kind could be heard.
You looked on amazed, and began to suspect yourself
of being deaf—then the night came suddenly, and
struck you blind as well. About three in the morning
some large fish leaped, and the loud splash made me
jump as though a gun had been fired. When the sun
rose there was a white fog, very warm and clammy,
and more blinding than the night. It did not shift or
drive; it was just there, standing all round you like
something solid. At eight or nine, perhaps, it lifted as
a shutter lifts. We had a glimpse of the towering multitude of trees, of the immense matted jungle, with the
blazing little ball of the sun hanging over it—all perfectly still—and then the white shutter came down
again, smoothly, as if sliding in greased grooves. I ordered the chain, which we had begun to heave in, to
be paid out again. Before it stopped running with a
muffled rattle, a cry, a very loud cry, as of infinite
desolation, soared slowly in the opaque air. It ceased.
A complaining clamour, modulated in savage discords,
filled our ears. The sheer unexpectedness of it made
my hair stir under my cap. I don't know how it struck
the others: to me it seemed as though the mist itself
had screamed, so suddenly, and apparently from all
sides at once, did this tumultuous and mournful uproar
arise. It culminated in a hurried outbreak of almost
intolerably excessive shrieking, which stopped short,
leaving us stiffened in a variety of silly attitudes, and
obstinately listening to the nearly as appalling and excessive silence. 'Good God! What is the meaning——'

stammered at my elbow one of the pilgrims—a little
fat man, with sandy hair and red whiskers, who wore
sidespring boots, and pink pyjamas tucked into his
socks. Two others remained open-mouthed a whole
minute, then dashed into the little cabin, to rush out
incontinently and stand darting scared glances, with
Winchesters at 'ready' in their hands. What we could
see was just the steamer we were on, her outlines
blurred as though she had been on the point of dis-
solving, and a misty strip of water, perhaps two feet
broad, around her—and that was all. The rest of the
world was nowhere, as far as our eyes and ears were
concerned. Just nowhere. Gone, disappeared; swept
off without leaving a whisper or a shadow behind.

   "I went forward, and ordered the chain to be hauled
in short, so as to be ready to trip the anchor and move
the steamboat at once if necessary. 'Will they attack?'
whispered an awed voice. 'We will be all butchered in
this fog,' murmured another. The faces twitched with
the strain, the hands trembled slightly, the eyes forgot
to wink. It was very curious to see the contrast of
expressions of the white men and of the black fellows
of our crew, who were as much strangers to that part
of the river as we, though their homes were only eight
hundred miles away. The whites, of course greatly dis-
composed, had besides a curious look of being painfully shocked by such an outrageous row. The others
had an alert, naturally interested expression; but their
faces were essentially quiet, even those of the one or
two who grinned as they hauled at the chain. Several
exchanged short, grunting phrases, which seemed to
settle the matter to their satisfaction. Their headman,
a young, broad-chested black, severely draped in dark-
blue fringed cloths, with fierce nostrils and his hair all
done up artfully in oily ringlets, stood near me. 'Aha!'
I said, just for good fellowship's sake. 'Catch 'im,' he
snapped, with a bloodshot widening of his eyes and a
flash of sharp teeth—'catch 'im. Give 'im to us.' 'To
you, eh?' I asked; 'what would you do with them?'
'Eat 'im!' he said curtly, and, leaning his elbow on the
rail, looked out into the fog in a dignified and pro-

foundly pensive attitude. I would no doubt have been properly horrified, had it not occurred to me that he and his chaps must be very hungry: that they must have been growing increasingly hungry for at least this month past. They had been engaged for six months (I don't think a single one of them had any clear idea of time, as we at the end of countless ages have. They still belonged to the beginnings of time—had no inherited experience to teach them as it were), and of course, as long as there was a piece of paper written over in accordance with some farcical law or other made down the river, it didn't enter anybody's head to trouble how they would live. Certainly they had brought with them some rotten hippo-meat, which couldn't have lasted very long, anyway, even if the pilgrims hadn't, in the midst of a shocking hullabaloo, thrown a considerable quantity of it overboard. It looked like a high-handed proceeding; but it was really a case of legitimate self-defence. You can't breathe dead hippo waking, sleeping, and eating, and at the same time keep your precarious grip on existence. Besides that, they had given them every week three pieces of brass wire, each about nine inches long; and the theory was they were to buy their provisions with that currency in riverside villages. You can see how *that* worked. There were either no villages, or the people were hostile, or the director, who like the rest of us fed out of tins, with an occasional old he-goat thrown in, didn't want to stop the steamer for some more or less recondite reason. So, unless they swallowed the wire itself, or made loops of it to snare the fishes with, I don't see what good their extravagant salary could do to them. I must say it was paid with a regularity worthy of a large and honourable trading company. For the rest, the only thing to eat—though it didn't look eatable in the least—I saw in their possession was a few lumps of some stuff like half-cooked dough, of a dirty lavender colour, they kept wrapped in leaves, and now and then swallowed a piece of, but so small that it seemed done more for the looks of the thing than for any serious purpose of sustenance.

Why in the name of all the gnawing devils of hunger they didn't go for us—they were thirty to five—and have a good tuck-in for once, amazes me now when I think of it. They were big powerful men, with no much capacity to weigh the consequences, with courage, with strength, even yet, though their skins were no longer glossy and their muscles no longer hard. And I saw that something restraining, one of those human secrets that baffle probability, had come into play there. I looked at them with a swift quickening of interest—not because it occurred to me I might be eaten by them before very long, though I own to you that just then I perceived—in a new light, as it were— how unwholesome the pilgrims looked, and I hoped, yes, I positively hoped, that my aspect was not so— what shall I say?—so—unappetizing: a touch of fantastic vanity which fitted well with the dream-sensation that pervaded all my days at that time. Perhaps I had a little fever, too. One can't live with one's finger ever-lastingly on one's pulse. I had often 'a little fever,' or a little touch of other things—the playful paw-strokes of the wilderness, the preliminary trifling before the more serious onslaught which came in due course. Yes; I looked at them as you would on any human being, with a curiosity of their impulses, motives, capacities, weaknesses, when brought to the test of an inexorable physical necessity. Restraint! What possible restraint? Was it superstition, disgust, patience, fear— or some kind of primitive honour? No fear can stand up to hunger, no patience can wear it out, disgust simply does not exist where hunger is; and as to superstition, beliefs, and what you may call principles, they are less than chaff in a breeze. Don't you know the devilry of lingering starvation, its exasperating torment, its black thoughts, its sombre and brooding ferocity? Well, I do. It takes a man all his inborn strength to fight hunger properly. It's really easier to face bereavement, dishonour, and the perdition of one's soul—than this kind of prolonged hunger. Sad, but true. And these chaps, too, had no earthly reason for any kind of scruple. Restraint! I would just as soon

have expected restraint from a hyena prowling
amongst the corpses of a battlefield. But there was the
fact facing me—the fact dazzling, to be seen, like the
foam on the depths of the sea, like a ripple on an
unfathomable enigma, a mystery greater—when I
thought of it—than the curious, inexplicable note of
desperate grief in this savage clamour that had swept
by us on the river-bank, behind the blind whiteness
of the fog.

"Two pilgrims were quarrelling in hurried whispers
as to which bank. 'Left.' 'No, no; how can you? Right,
right, of course.' 'It is very serious,' said the manager's
voice behind me; 'I would be desolated if anything
should happen to Mr. Kurtz before we came up.' I
looked at him, and had not the slightest doubt he was
sincere. He was just the kind of man who would wish
to preserve appearances. That was his restraint. But
when he muttered something about going on at once,
I did not even take the trouble to answer him. I knew,
and he knew, that it was impossible. Were we to let
go our hold of the bottom, we would be absolutely in
the air—in space. We wouldn't be able to tell where
we were going to—whether up or down stream, or
across—till we fetched against one bank or the
other—and then we wouldn't know at first which it
was. Of course I made no move. I had no mind for a
smash-up. You couldn't imagine a more deadly place
for a shipwreck. Whether drowned at once or not, we
were sure to perish speedily in one way or another. 'I
authorize you to take all the risks,' he said, after a
short silence. 'I refuse to take any,' I said shortly;
which was just the answer he expected, though its tone
might have surprised him. 'Well, I must defer to your
judgment. You are captain,' he said with marked civ-
ilty. I turned my shoulder to him in sign of my appreciation, and looked into the fog. How long would
it last? It was the most hopeless lookout. The approach to this Kurtz grubbing for ivory in the
wretched bush was beset by as many dangers as
though he had been an enchanted princess sleeping in

a fabulous castle. "Will they attack, do you think?" asked the manager, in a confidential tone.

"I did not think they would attack, for several obvious reasons. The thick fog was one. If they left the bank in their canoes they would get lost in it, as we would be if we attempted to move. Still, I had also judged the jungle of both banks quite impenetrable—and yet eyes were in it, eyes that had seen us. The riverside bushes were certainly very thick; but the undergrowth behind was evidently penetrable. However, during the short lift I had seen no canoes anywhere in the reach—certainly not abreast of the steamer. But what made the idea of attack inconceivable to me was the nature of the noise—of the cries we had heard. They had not the fierce character boding immediate hostile intention. Unexpected, wild, and violent as they had been, they had given me an irresistible impression of sorrow. The glimpse of the steamboat had for some reason filled those savages with unrestrained grief. The danger, if any, I expounded, was from our proximity to a great human passion let loose. Even extreme grief may ultimately vent itself in violence—but more generally takes the form of apathy. . . .

"You should have seen the pilgrims stare! They had no heart to grin, or even to revile me: but I believe they thought me gone mad—with fright, maybe. I delivered a regular lecture. My dear boys, it was no good bothering. Keep a lookout? Well, you may guess I watched the fog for the signs of lifting as a cat watches a mouse; but for anything else were of no more use to us than if we had been buried miles deep in a heap of cotton-wool. It felt like it, too—choking, warm, stifling. Besides, all I said, though it sounded extravagant, was absolutely true to fact. What we afterwards alluded to as an attack was really an attempt to repulse. The action was very far from being aggressive—it was not even defensive, in the usual sense: it was undertaken under the stress of desperation, and in its essence was purely protective.

"It developed itself, I should say, two hours after the fog lifted, and its commencement was at a spot,

roughly speaking, about a mile and a half below
Kurtz's station. We had just floundered and flopped
round a bend, when I saw an islet, a mere grassy hum-
mock of bright green, in the middle of the stream. It
was the only thing of the kind; but as we opened the
reach more, I perceived it was the head of a long
sand-bank, or rather of a chain of shallow patches
stretching down the middle of the river. They were
discoloured, just awash, and the whole lot was seen
just under the water, exactly as a man's backbone is
seen running down the middle of his back under the
skin. Now, as far as I did see, I could go to the right
or to the left of this. I didn't know either channel, of
course. The banks looked pretty well alike, the depth
appeared the same; but as I had been informed the
station was on the west side, I naturally headed for
the western passage.

"No sooner had we fairly entered it than I became
aware it was much narrower than I had supposed. To
the left of us there was the long uninterrupted shoal,
and to the right a high, steep bank heavily overgrown
with bushes. Above the bush the trees stood in serried
ranks. The twigs overhung the current thickly, and
from distance to distance a large limb of some tree
projected rigidly over the stream. It was then well on
in the afternoon, the face of the forest was gloomy,
and a broad strip of shadow had already fallen on the
water. In this shadow we steamed up—very slowly, as
you may imagine. I sheered her well inshore—the
water being deepest near the bank, as the sounding-
pole informed me.

"One of my hungry and forbearing friends was
sounding in the bows just below me. This steamboat
was exactly like a decked scow. On the deck, there
were two little teakwood houses, with doors and windows. The boiler was in the fore-end, and the machinery right astern. Over the whole there was a light roof,
supported on stanchions. The funnel projected
through that roof, and in front of the funnel a small
cabin built of light planks served for a pilot-house. It
contained a couch, two camp-stools, a loaded Martini-

Henry leaning in one corner, a tiny table, and the steering-wheel. It had a wide door in front and a broad shutter at each side. All these were always thrown open, of course. I spent my days perched up there on the extreme fore-end of that roof, before the door. At night I slept, or tried to, on the couch. An athletic black belonging to some coast tribe and educated by my poor predecessor, was the helmsman. He sported a pair of brass earrings, wore a blue cloth wrapper from the waist to the ankles, and thought all the world of himself. He was the most unstable kind of fool I had ever seen. He steered with no end of a swagger while you were by; but if he lost sight of you, he became instantly the prey of an abject funk, and would let that cripple of a steamboat get the upper hand of him in a minute.

"I was looking down at the sounding-pole, and feeling much annoyed to see at each try a little more of it stick out of that river, when I saw my poleman give up the business suddenly, and stretch himself flat on the deck, without even taking the trouble to haul his pole in. He kept hold on it though, and it trailed in the water. At the same time the fireman, whom I could also see below me, sat down abruptly before his furnace and ducked his head. I was amazed. Then I had to look at the river mighty quick, because there was a snag in the fairway. Sticks, little sticks, were flying about—thick: they were whizzing before my nose, dropping below me, striking behind me against my pilot-house. All this time the river, the shore, the woods, were very quiet—perfectly quiet. I could only hear the heavy splashing thump of the stern-wheel and the patter of these things. We cleared the snag clumsily. Arrows, by Jove! We were being shot at! I stepped in quickly to close the shutter on the landside. That fool-helmsman, his hands on the spokes, was lifting his knees high, stamping his feet, champing his mouth, like a reined-in horse. Confound him! And we were staggering within ten feet of the bank. I had to lean right out to swing the heavy shutter, and I saw a face amongst the leaves on the level with my own,

looking at me very fierce and steady; and then suddenly, as though a veil had been removed from my
eyes, I made out, deep in the tangled gloom, naked
breasts, arms, legs, glaring eyes—the bush was swarm-
ing with human limbs in movement, glistening, of
bronze colour. The twigs shook, swayed, and rustled,
the arrows flew out of them, and then the shutter came
to. 'Steer her straight,' I said to the helmsman. He
held his head rigid, face forward; but his eyes rolled,
he kept on lifting and setting down his feet gently,
his mouth foamed a little. 'Keep quiet!' I said in a fury.
I might just as well have ordered a tree not to sway
in the wind. I darted out. Below me there was a great
scuffle of feet on the iron deck; confused exclamations;
a voice screamed, 'Can you turn back?' I caught sight
of a V-shaped ripple on the water ahead. What? Another snag? A fusillade burst out under my feet. The
pilgrims had opened with their Winchesters, and were
simply squirting lead into that bush. A deuce of a lot
of smoke came up and drove slowly forward. I swore
at it. Now I couldn't see the ripple or the snag either.
I stood in the doorway, peering, and the arrows came
in swarms. They might have been poisoned, but they
looked as though they wouldn't kill a cat. The bush
began to howl. Our wood-cutters raised a warlike
whoop; the report of a rifle just at my back deafened
me. I glanced over my shoulder, and the pilot-house
was yet full of noise and smoke when I made a dash
at the wheel. The fool-nigger had dropped everything,
to throw the shutter open and let off that Martini-
Henry. He stood before the wide opening, glaring, and
I yelled at him to come back, while I straightened the
sudden twist out of that steamboat. There was no
room to turn even if I had wanted to, the snag was
somewhere very near ahead in that confounded
smoke, there was no time to lose, so I just crowded
her into the bank—right into the bank, where I knew
the water was deep.

"We tore slowly along the overhanging bushes in a
whirl of broken twigs and flying leaves. The fusillade
below stopped short, as I had foreseen it would when

the squirts got empty. I threw my head back to a glinting whizz that traversed the pilot-house, in at one shutter-hole and out at the other. Looking past that mad helmsman, who was shaking the empty rifle and yelling at the shore, I saw vague forms of men running bent double, leaping, gliding, distinct, incomplete, evanescent. Something big appeared in the air before the shutter, the rifle went overboard, and the man stepped back swiftly, looked at me over his shoulder in an extraordinary, profound, familiar manner, and fell upon my feet. The side of his head hit the wheel twice, and the end of what appeared a long cane clattered round and knocked over a little camp-stool. It looked as though after wrenching that thing from somebody ashore he had lost his balance in the effort. The thin smoke had blown away, we were clear of the snag, and looking ahead I could see that in another hundred yards or so I would be free to sheer off, away from the bank; but my feet felt so very warm and wet that I had to look down. The man had rolled on his back and stared straight up at me; both his hands clutched that cane. It was the shaft of a spear that, either thrown or lunged through the opening, had caught him in the side just below the ribs; the blade had gone in out of sight, after making a frightful gash; my shoes were full; a pool of blood lay very still, gleaming dark-red under the wheel; his eyes shone with an amazing lustre. The fusillade burst out again. He looked at me anxiously, gripping the spear like something precious, with an air of being afraid I would try to take it away from him. I had to make an effort to free my eyes from his gaze and attend to the steering. With one hand I felt above my head for the line of the steam whistle, and jerked out screech after screech hurriedly. The tumult of angry and warlike yells was checked instantly, and then from the depths of the woods went out such a tremulous and prolonged wail of mournful fear and utter despair as may be imagined to follow the flight of the last hope from the earth. There was a great commotion in the bush; the shower of arrows stopped, a few dropping shots rang out sharply—then silence, in which the languid beat of the stern-wheel came plainly to my ears. I put the helm hard a-starboard at the moment when the pilgrim in pink pyjamas, very hot and agitated, appeared in the doorway. 'The manager sends me——' he began in an official tone, and stopped short. 'Good God!'' he said, glaring at the wounded man.

"We two whites stood over him, and his lustrous and inquiring glance enveloped us both. I declare it looked as though he would presently put to us some question in an understandable language; but he died without uttering a sound, without moving a limb, without twitching a muscle. Only in the very last moment, as though in response to some sign we could not see, to some whisper we could not hear, he frowned heavily, and that frown gave to his black death-mask an inconceivably sombre, brooding, and menacing expression. The lustre of inquiring glance faded swiftly into vacant glassiness. 'Can you steer?' I asked the agent eagerly. He looked very dubious; but I made a grab at his arm, and he understood at once I meant him to steer whether or no. To tell you the truth, I was morbidly anxious to change my shoes and socks. 'He is dead,' murmured the fellow, immensely impressed. 'No doubt about it,' said I, tugging like mad at the shoe-laces. 'And by the way, I suppose Mr. Kurtz is dead as well by this time.'

"For the moment that was the dominant thought. There was a sense of extreme disappointment, as though I had found out I had been striving after something altogether without a substance. I couldn't have been more disgusted if I had travelled all this way for the sole purpose of talking with Mr. Kurtz. Talking with . . . I flung one shoe overboard, and became aware that that was exactly what I had been looking forward to—a talk with Kurtz. I made the strange discovery that I had never imagined him as doing, you know, but as discoursing. I didn't say to myself, 'Now I will never see him,' or 'Now I will never shake him by the hand,' but, 'Now I will never hear him.' The man presented himself as a voice. Not of course that

I did not connect him with some sort of action. Hadn't I been told in all the tones of jealousy and admiration that he had collected, bartered, swindled, or stolen more ivory than all the other agents together? That was not the point. The point was in his being a gifted creature, and that of all his gifts the one that stood out preëminently, that carried with it a sense of real presence, was his ability to talk, his words—the gift of expression, the bewildering, the illuminating, the most exalted and the most contemptible, the pulsating stream of light, or the deceitful flow from the heart of an impenetrable darkness.

"The other shoe went flying unto the devil-god of that river. I thought, 'By Jove! it's all over. We are too late; he has vanished—the gift has vanished, by means of some spear, arrow, or club. I will never hear that chap speak after all'—and my sorrow had a startling extravagance of emotion, even such as I had noticed in the howling sorrow of these savages in the bush. I couldn't have felt more of lonely desolation somehow, had I been robbed of a belief or had missed my destiny in life. . . . Why do you sigh in this beastly way, somebody? Absurd? Well, absurd. Good Lord! mustn't a man ever——Here, give me some tobacco." . . .

There was a pause of profound stillness, then a match flared, and Marlow's lean face appeared, worn, hollow, with downward folds and dropped eyelids, with an aspect of concentrated attention; and as he took vigorous draws at his pipe, it seemed to retreat and advance out of the night in the regular flicker of tiny flame. The match went out.

"Absurd!" he cried. "This is the worst of trying to tell. . . . Here you all are, each moored with two good addresses, like a hulk with two anchors, a butcher round one corner, a policeman round another, excellent appetites, and temperature normal—you hear—normal from year's end to year's end. And you say, Absurd! Absurd be—exploded! Absurd! My dear boys, what can you expect from a man who out of sheer nervousness had just flung overboard a pair of

new shoes! Now I think of it, it is amazing I did not
shed tears. I am, upon the whole, proud of my forti-
tude. I was cut to the quick at the idea of having lost
the inestimable privilege of listening to the gifted
Kurtz. Of course I was wrong. The privilege was waiting for me. Oh, yes, I heard more than enough. And
I was right, too. A voice. He was very little more
than a voice. And I heard—him—it—this voice—other
voices—all of them were so little more than voices—
and the memory of that time itself lingers around me,
impalpable, like a dying vibration of one immense jab-
ber, silly, atrocious, sordid, savage, or simply mean,
without any kind of sense. Voices, voices—even the
girl herself—now——"

He was silent for a long time.

"I laid the ghost of his gifts at last with a lie," he
began, suddenly. "Girl! What? Did I mention a girl?
Oh, she is out of it—completely. They—the women I
mean—are out of it—should be out of it. We must
help them to stay in that beautiful world of their own,
lest ours gets worse. Oh, she had to be out of it. You
should have heard the disinterred body of Mr. Kurtz
saying, 'My Intended.' You would have perceived directly then how completely she was out of it. And the
lofty frontal bone of Mr. Kurtz! They say the hair
goes on growing sometimes, but this—ah—specimen,
was impressively bald. The wilderness had patted him
on the head, and, behold, it was like a ball—an ivory
ball; it had caressed him, and—lo!—he had withered;
it had taken him, loved him, embraced him, got into
his veins, consumed his flesh, and sealed his soul to its
own by the inconceivable ceremonies of some devilish
initiation. He was its spoiled and pampered favourite.
Ivory? I should think so. Heaps of it, stacks of it. The
old mud shanty was bursting with it. You would think
there was not a single tusk left either above or below
the ground in the whole country. 'Mostly fossil,' the
manager had remarked, disparagingly. It was no more
fossil than I am; but they call it fossil when it is dug
up. It appears these niggers do bury the tusks sometimes—but evidently they couldn't bury this parcel

deep enough to save the gifted Mr. Kurtz from his fate.
We filled the steamboat with it, and had to pile a lot on
the deck. Thus he could see and enjoy as long as he
could see, because the appreciation of this favour had
remained with him to the last. You should have heard
him say, 'My ivory.' Oh, yes, I heard him. 'My Intended,
my ivory, my station, my river, my——' everything belonged to him. It made me hold my breath in expectation of hearing the wilderness burst into a prodigious
peal of laughter that would shake the fixed stars in
their places. Everything belonged to him—but that
was a trifle. The thing was to know what he belonged
to, how many powers of darkness claimed him for
their own. That was the reflection that made you
creepy all over. It was impossible—it was not good
for one either—trying to imagine. He had taken a high
seat amongst the devils of the land—I mean literally.
You can't understand. How could you?—with solid
pavement under your feet, surrounded by kind
neighbours ready to cheer you or to fall on you, step-
ping delicately between the butcher and the policeman, in the holy terror of scandal and gallows and
lunatic asylums—how can you imagine what particular
region of the first ages a man's untrammelled feet may
take him into by the way of solitude—utter solitude
without a policeman—by the way of silence—utter silence, where no warning voice of a kind neighbour
can be heard whispering of public opinion? These little things make all the great difference. When they
are gone you must fall back upon your own innate
strength, upon your own capacity for faithfulness. Of
course you may be too much of a fool to go wrong—
too dull even to know you are being assaulted by the
powers of darkness. I take it, no fool ever made a
bargain for his soul with the devil; the fool is too much
of a fool, or the devil too much of a devil—I don't
know which. Or you may be such a thunderingly exalted creature as to be altogether deaf and blind to
anything but heavenly sights and sounds. Then the
earth for you is only a standing place—and whether
to be like this is your loss or your gain I won't pretend

to say. But most of us are neither one nor the other.
The earth for us is a place to live in, where we must
put up with sights, with sounds, with smells, too, by
Jove!—breathe dead hippo, so to speak, and not be
contaminated. And there, don't you see? Your
strength comes in, the faith in your ability for the
digging of unostentatious holes to bury the stuff in—
your power of devotion, not to yourself, but to an
obscure, back-breaking business. And that's difficult
enough. Mind, I am not trying to excuse or even explain—I am trying to account to myself for—for—Mr.
Kurtz—for the shade of Mr. Kurtz. This initiated
wraith from the back of Nowhere honoured me with
its amazing confidence before it vanished altogether.
This was because it could speak English to me. The
original Kurtz had been educated partly in England,
and—as he was good enough to say himself—his sym-
pathies were in the right place. His mother was half-
English, his father was half-French. All Europe con-
tributed to the making of Kurtz; and by and by I
learned that, most appropriately, the International Society for the Suppression of Savage Customs had intrusted him with the making of a report, for its future
guidance. And he had written it, too. I've seen it. I've
read it. It was eloquent, vibrating with eloquence, but
too high-strung, I think. Seventeen pages of close writing he had found time for! But this must have been
before his—let us say—nerves, went wrong, and
caused him to preside at certain midnight dances ending with unspeakable rites, which—as far as I reluc-
tantly gathered from what I heard at various times—
were offered up to him—do you understand?—to Mr.
Kurtz himself. But it was a beautiful piece of writing.
The opening paragraph, however, in the light of later
information, strikes me now as ominous. He began
with the argument that we whites, from the point of
development we had arrived at, 'must necessarily appear to them [savages] in the nature of supernatural
beings—we approach them with the might as of a
deity,' and so on, and so on. 'By the simple exercise
of our will we can exert a power for good practically

unbounded,' etc., etc. From that point he soared and took me with him. The peroration was magnificent, though difficult to remember, you know. It gave me the notion of an exotic Immensity ruled by an august Benevolence. It made me tingle with enthusiasm. This was the unbounded power of eloquence—of words— of burning noble words. There were no practical hints to interrupt the magic current of phrases, unless a kind of note at the foot of the last page, scrawled evidently much later, in an unsteady hand, may be regarded as the exposition of a method. It was very simple, and at the end of that moving appeal to every altruistic senti- ment it blazed at you, luminous and terrifying, like a flash of lightning in a serene sky: 'Exterminate all the brutes!' The curious part was that he had apparently forgotten all about that valuable postscriptum, be- cause, later on, when he in a sense came to himself, he repeatedly entreated me to take good care of 'my pamphlet' (he called it), as it was sure to have in the future a good influence upon his career. I had full information about all these things, and, besides, as it turned out, I was to have the care of his memory. I've done enough for it to give me the indisputable right to lay it, if I choose, for an everlasting rest in the dust-bin of progress, amongst all the sweepings and, figuratively speaking, all the dead cats of civilization. But then, you see, I can't choose. He won't be forgot- ten. Whatever he was, he was not common. He had the power to charm or frighten rudimentary souls into an aggravated witch-dance in his honour; he could also fill the small souls of the pilgrims with bitter misgiv- ings: he had one devoted friend at least, and he had conquered one soul in the world that was neither rudi- mentary nor tainted with self-seeking. No; I can't for- get him, though I am not prepared to affirm the fellow was exactly worth the life we lost in getting to him. I missed my late helmsman awfully—I missed him even while his body was still lying in the pilot-house. Per- haps you will think it passing strange this regret for a savage who was no more account than a grain of sand in a black Sahara. Well, don't you see, he had done something, he had steered; for months I had him at my back—a help—an instrument. It was a kind of partnership. He steered for me—I had to look after him, I worried about his deficiencies, and thus a subtle bond had been created, of which I only became aware when it was suddenly broken. And the intimate profundity of that look he gave me when he received his hurt remains to this day in my memory—like a claim of distant kinship affirmed in a supreme moment.

"Poor fool! If he had only left that shutter alone. He had no restraint, no restraint—just like Kurtz—a tree swayed by the wind. As soon as I had put on a dry pair of slippers, I dragged him out, after first jerking the spear out of his side, which operation I confess I performed with my eyes shut tight. His heels leaped together over the little doorstep; his shoulders were pressed to my breast; I hugged him from behind desperately. Oh! he was heavy, heavy; heavier than any man on earth, I should imagine. Then without more ado I tipped him overboard. The current snatched him as though he had been a wisp of grass, and I saw the body roll over twice before I lost sight of it for ever. All the pilgrims and the manager were then congregated on the awning-deck about the pilot-house, chattering at each other like a flock of excited magpies, and there was a scandalized murmur at my heartless promptitude. What they wanted to keep that body hanging about for I can't guess. Embalm it, maybe. But I had also heard another, and a very ominous, murmur on the deck below. My friends the woodcutters were likewise scandalized, and with a better show of reason—though I admit that the reason itself was quite inadmissible. Oh, quite! I had made up my mind that if my late helmsman was to be eaten, the fishes alone should have him. He had been a very second-rate helmsman while alive, but now he was dead he might have become a first-class temptation, and possibly cause some startling trouble. Besides, I was anxious to take the wheel, the man in pink pyjamas showing himself a hopeless duffer at the business.

"This I did directly the simple funeral was over. We

were going half-speed, keeping right in the middle of
the stream, and I listened to the talk about me. They
had given up Kurtz, they had given up the station;
Kurtz was dead, and the station had been burnt—and
so on—and so on. The red-haired pilgrim was beside
himself with the thought that at least this poor Kurtz
had been properly avenged. 'Say! We must have made
a glorious slaughter of them in the bush. Eh? What
do you think? Say?' He positively danced, the blood-
thirsty little gingery beggar. And he had nearly fainted
when he saw the wounded man! I could not help saying, 'You made a glorious lot of smoke, anyhow.' I
had seen, from the way the tops of bushes rustled and
flew, that almost all the shots had gone too high. You
can't hit anything unless you take aim and fire from
the shoulder; but these chaps fired from the hip with
their eyes shut. The retreat, I maintained—and I was
right—was caused by the screeching of the steam whistle. Upon this they forgot Kurtz, and began to howl
at me with indignant protests.

"The manager stood by the wheel murmuring con-
fidentially about the necessity of getting well away
down the river before dark at all events, when I saw
in the distance a clearing on the riverside and the
outlines of some sort of building. 'What's this?' I
asked. He clapped his hands in wonder. 'The station!'
he cried. I edged in at once, still going half-speed.

"Through my glasses I saw the slope of a hill inter-
spersed with rare trees and perfectly free from undergrowth. A long decaying building on the summit was
half buried in the high grass; the large holes in the
peaked roof gaped black from afar; the jungle and the
woods made a background. There was no enclosure
or fence of any kind; but there had been one apparently, for near the house half-a-dozen slim posts remained in a row, roughly trimmed, and with their
upper ends ornamented with round carved balls. The
rails, or whatever there had been between, had disappeared. Of course the forest surrounded all that. The
river-bank was clear, and on the waterside I saw a
white man under a hat like a cart-wheel beckoning

persistently with his whole arm. Examining the edge of the forest above and below, I was almost certain I could see movements—human forms gliding here and there. I steamed past prudently, then stopped the engines and let her drift down. The man on the shore began to shout, urging us to land. 'We have been attacked,' screamed the manager. 'I know—I know. It's all right,' yelled back the other, as cheerful as you please. 'Come along. It's all right. I am glad.'

"His aspect reminded me of something I had seen—something funny I had seen somewhere. As I manœuvred to get alongside, I was asking myself, 'What does this fellow look like?' Suddenly I got it. He looked like a harlequin. His clothes had been made of some stuff that was brown holland probably, but it was covered with patches all over, with bright patches, blue, red, and yellow—patches on the back, patches on the front, patches on elbows, on knees; coloured binding around his jacket, scarlet edging at the bottom of his trousers; and the sunshine made him look extremely gay and wonderfully neat withal, because you could see how beautifully all this patching had been done. A beardless, boyish face, very fair, no features to speak of, nose peeling, little blue eyes, smiles and frowns chasing each other over that open countenance like sunshine and shadow on a wind-swept plain. 'Look out, captain!' he cried; 'there's a snag lodged in here last night.' What! Another snag? I confess I swore shamefully. I had nearly holed my cripple, to finish off that charming trip. The harlequin on the bank turned his little pug-nose up to me. 'You English?' he asked, all smiles. 'Are you?' I shouted from the wheel. The smiles vanished, and he shook his head as if sorry for my disappointment. Then he brightened up. 'Never mind!' he cried encouragingly. 'Are we in time?' I asked. 'He is up there,' he replied, with a toss of the head up the hill, and becoming gloomy all of a sudden. His face was like the autumn sky, overcast one moment and bright the next.

"When the manager, escorted by the pilgrims, all of them armed to the teeth, had gone to the house this

chap came on board. 'I say, I don't like this. These
natives are in the bush,' I said. He assured me earnestly it was all right. 'They are simple people,' he
added; 'well, I am glad you came. It took me all my
time to keep them off.' 'But you said it was all right,'
I cried. 'Oh, they meant no harm,' he said; and as I
stared he corrected himself, 'Not exactly.' Then viva-
ciously, 'My faith, your pilot-house wants a clean-up!'
In the next breath he advised me to keep enough
steam on the boiler to blow the whistle in case of any
trouble. 'One good screech will do more for you than
all your rifles. They are simple people,' he repeated.
He rattled away at such a rate he quite overwhelmed
me. He seemed to be trying to make up for lots of
silence, and actually hinted, laughing, that such was the
case. 'Don't you talk with Mr. Kurtz?' I said. 'You don't
talk with that man—you listen to him,' he exclaimed
with severe exaltation. 'But now——' He waved his arm,
and in the twinkling of an eye was in the uttermost
depths of despondency. In a moment he came up again
with a jump, possessed himself of both my hands, shook
them continuously, while he gabbled: 'Brother sailor . . .
honour . . . pleasure . . . delight . . . introduce myself . . .
Russian . . . son of an arch-priest . . . Government of
Tambov . . . What? Tobacco! English tobacco; the excellent English tobacco! Now, that's brotherly. Smoke?
Where's a sailor that does not smoke?"

"The pipe soothed him, and gradually I made out
he had run away from school, had gone to sea in a
Russian ship; ran away again; served some time in
English ships; was now reconciled with the arch-priest.
He made a point of that. 'But when one is young one
must see things, gather experience, ideas; enlarge the
mind.' 'Here!' I interrupted. 'You can never tell! Here
I met Mr. Kurtz,' he said, youthfully solemn and re-
proachful. I held my tongue after that. It appears he
had persuaded a Dutch trading-house on the coast to
fit him out with stores and goods, and had started for
the interior with a light heart and no more idea of
what would happen to him than a baby. He had been
wandering about that river for nearly two years alone,

cut off from everybody and everything. 'I am not so young as I look. I am twenty-five,' he said. 'At first old Van Shuyten would tell me to go to the devil,' he narrated with keen enjoyment; 'but I stuck to him, and talked and talked, till at last he got afraid I would talk the hind-leg off his favourite dog, so he gave me some cheap things and a few guns, and told me he hoped he would never see my face again. Good old Dutchman, Van Shuyten. I've sent him one small lot of ivory a year ago, so that he can't call me a little thief when I get back. I hope he got it. And for the rest I don't care. I had some wood stacked for you. That was my old house. Did you see?'

"I gave him Towson's book. He made as though he would kiss me, but restrained himself. 'The only book I had left, and I thought I had lost it,' he said, looking at it ecstatically. 'So many accidents happen to a man going about alone, you know. Canoes get upset sometimes— and sometimes you've got to clear out so quick when the people get angry.' He thumbed the pages. 'You made notes in Russian?' I asked. He nodded. 'I thought they were written in cipher,' I said. He laughed, then became serious. 'I had lots of trouble to keep these people off,' he said. 'Did they want to kill you?' I asked. 'Oh, no!' he cried, and checked himself. 'Why did they attack us?' I pursued. He hesitated, then said shame-facedly, 'They don't want him to go.' 'Don't they?' I said curiously. He nodded a nod full of mystery and wisdom. 'I tell you,' he cried, 'this man has enlarged my mind.' He opened his arms wide, staring at me with his little blue eyes that were perfectly round.

III

"I looked at him, lost in astonishment. There he was before me, in motley, as though he had absconded from a troupe of mimes, enthusiastic, fabulous. His very existence was improbable, inexplicable, and alto-gether bewildering. He was an insoluble problem. It was inconceivable how he had existed, how he had succeeded in getting so far, how he had managed to remain—why he did not instantly disappear. 'I went a little farther,' he said, 'then still a little farther—till I had gone so far that I don't know how I'll ever get back. Never mind. Plenty time. I can manage. You take Kurtz away quick—quick—I tell you.' The glamour of youth enveloped his parti-coloured rags, his destitution, his loneliness, the essential desolation of his futile wanderings. For months—for years—his life hadn't been worth a day's purchase; and there he was gallantly, thoughtlessly alive, to all appearance indestructible solely by the virtue of his few years and of his unreflecting audacity. I was seduced into something like admiration—like envy. Glamour urged him on, glamour kept him unscathed. He surely wanted nothing from the wilderness but space to breathe in and to push on through. His need was to exist, and to move onwards at the greatest possible risk, and with a maximum of privation. If the absolutely pure, uncalculating, unpractical spirit of adventure had ever ruled a human being, it ruled this bepatched youth. I almost envied him the possession of this modest and clear flame. It seemed to have consumed all thought of self so completely, that even while he was talking to you, you forgot that it was he—the man before your eyes—who had gone through these things. I did not envy him his devotion to Kurtz, though. He had not meditated over it. It came to him, and he accepted it with a sort of eager fatalism. I must say that to me it appeared about the most dangerous thing in every way he had come upon so far.

"They had come together unavoidably, like two ships becalmed near each other, and lay rubbing sides at last. I suppose Kurtz wanted an audience, because on a certain occasion, when encamped in the forest, they had talked all night, or more probably Kurtz had talked. 'We talked of everything,' he said, quite transported at the recollection. 'I forgot there was such a thing as sleep. The night did not seem to last an hour. Everything! Everything! . . . Of love, too.' 'Ah, he talked to you of love!' I said, much amused. 'It isn't what you think,' he cried, almost passionately. 'It was in general. He made me see things—things.'

"He threw his arms up. We were on deck at the time, and the headman of my wood-cutters, lounging near by, turned upon him his heavy and glittering eyes. I looked around, and I don't know why, but I assure you that never, never before, did this land, this river, this jungle, the very arch of this blazing sky, appear to me so hopeless and so dark, so impenetrable to human thought, so pitiless to human weakness. 'And, ever since, you have been with him, of course?' I said.

"On the contrary. It appears their intercourse had been very much broken by various causes. He had, as he informed me proudly, managed to nurse Kurtz through two illnesses (he alluded to it as you would to some risky feat), but as a rule Kurtz wandered alone, far in the depths of the forest. 'Very often coming to this station, I had to wait days and days before he would turn up,' he said. 'Ah, it was worth waiting for!—sometimes.' 'What was he doing? exploring or what?' I asked. 'Oh, yes, of course'; he had discovered lots of villages, a lake, too—he did not know exactly in what direction; it was dangerous to inquire too much—but mostly his expeditions had been for ivory. 'But he had no goods to trade with by that time,' I objected. 'There's a good lot of cartridges left even yet,' he answered, looking away. 'To speak plainly, he raided the country,' I said. He nodded. 'Not alone, surely!' He muttered something about the villages round that lake. 'Kurtz got the tribe to follow him, did he?' I suggested. He fidgeted a little. 'They adored him,' he said. The tone of these words was so extraordinary that I looked at him searchingly. It was curious to see his mingled eagerness and reluctance to speak of Kurtz. The man filled his life, occupied his thoughts, swayed his emotions. 'What can you expect?' he burst out; 'he came to them with thunder and lightning, you know—and they had never seen anything like it—and very terrible. He could be very terrible. You can't judge Mr. Kurtz as you would an ordinary man. No,

no, no! Now—just to give you an idea—I don't mind
telling you, he wanted to shoot me, too, one day—but
I don't judge him.' 'Shoot you!' I cried. 'What for?'
'Well, I had a small lot of ivory the chief of that village
near my house gave me. You see I used to shoot game
for them. Well, he wanted it, and wouldn't hear reason. He declared he would shoot me unless I gave
him the ivory and then cleared out of the country,
because he could do so, and had a fancy for it, and
there was nothing on earth to prevent him killing
whom he jolly well pleased. And it was true, too. I
gave him the ivory. What did I care! But I didn't clear
out. No, no. I couldn't leave him. I had to be careful,
of course, till we got friendly again for a time. He had
his second illness then. Afterwards I had to keep out
of the way; but I didn't mind. He was living for the
most part in those villages on the lake. When he came
down to the river, sometimes he would take to me,
and sometimes it was better for me to be careful. This
man suffered too much. He hated all this, and somehow he couldn't get away. When I had a chance I
begged him to try and leave while there was time; I
offered to go back with him. And he would say yes,
and then he would remain; go off on another ivory
hunt; disappear for weeks; forget himself amongst
these people—forget himself—you know.' 'Why! he's
mad,' I said. He protested indignantly. Mr. Kurtz
couldn't be mad. If I had heard him talk, only two
days ago, I wouldn't dare hint at such a thing. . . . I
had take up my binoculars while we talked, and was
looking at the shore, sweeping the limit of the forest
at each side and at the back of the house. The con-
sciousness of there being people in that bush, so silent,
so quiet—as silent and quiet as the ruined house on
the hill—made me uneasy. There was no sign on the
face of nature of this amazing tale that was not so
much told as suggested to me in desolate exclamations, completed by shrugs, in interrupted phrases, in
hints ending in deep sighs. The woods were unmoved,
like a mask—heavy, like the closed door of a prison—
they looked with their air of hidden knowledge, of

patient expectation, of unapproachable silence. The
Russian was explaining to me that it was only lately
that Mr. Kurtz had come down to the river, bringing
along with him all the fighting men of that lake tribe.
He had been absent for several months—getting himself adored, I suppose—and had come down unexpectedly, with the intention to all appearance of making
a raid either across the river or down stream. Evidently the appetite for more ivory had got the better
of the—what shall I say?—less material aspirations.
However he had got much worse suddenly. 'I heard
he was lying helpless, and so I came up—took my
chance,' said the Russian. 'Oh, he is bad, very bad.' I
directed my glass to the house. There were no signs
of life, but there was the ruined roof, the long mud
wall peeping above the grass, with three little square
window-holes, no two of the same size; all this brought
within reach of my hand, as it were. And then I made
a brusque movement, and one of the remaining posts
of that vanished fence leaped up in the field of my
glass. You remember I told you I had been struck at
the distance but certain attempts at ornamentation,
rather remarkable in the ruinous aspect of the place.
Now I had suddenly a nearer view, and its first result
was to make me throw my head back as if before a
blow. Then I went carefully from post to post with my
glass, and I saw my mistake. These round knobs were
not ornamental but symbolic; they were expressive and
puzzling, striking and disturbing—food for thought
and also for vultures if there had been any looking
down from the sky; but at all events for such ants as
were industrious enough to ascend the pole. They
would have been even more impressive, those heads
on the stakes, if their faces had not been turned to the
house. Only one, the first I had made out, was facing
my way. I was not so shocked as you may think. The
start back I had given was really nothing but a movement of surprise. I had expected to see a knob of
wood there, you know. I returned deliberately to the
first I had seen—and there it was, black, dried, sunken,
with closed eyelids—a head that seemed to sleep at

the top of that pole, and, with the shrunken dry lips
showing a narrow white line of the teeth, was smiling,
too, smiling continuously at some endless and jocose
dream of that eternal slumber.

"I am not disclosing any trade secrets. In fact, the
manager said afterwards that Mr. Kurtz's methods had
ruined the district. I have no opinion on that point,
but I want you clearly to understand that there was
nothing exactly profitable in these heads being there.
They only showed that Mr. Kurtz lacked restraint in
the gratification of his various lusts, that there was
something wanting in him—some small matter which,
when the pressing need arose, could not be found
under his magnificent eloquence. Whether he knew of
this deficiency himself I can't say. I think the knowledge came to him at last—only at the very last. But
the wilderness had found him out early, and had taken
on him a terrible vengeance for the fantastic invasion.
I think it had whispered to him things about himself
which he did not know, things of which he had no
conception till he took counsel with this great solitude—and the whisper had proved irresistibly fascinating. It echoed loudly within him because he was
hollow at the core. . . . I put down the glass, and the
head that had appeared near enough to be spoken to
seemed at once to have leaped away from me into
inaccessible distance.

"The admirer of Mr. Kurtz was a bit crestfallen. In
a hurried, indistinct voice he began to assure me he
had not dared to take these—say, symbols—down. He
was not afraid of the natives; they would not stir till
Mr. Kurtz gave the word. His ascendancy was extraordinary. The camps of these people surrounded the
place, and the chiefs came every day to see him. They
would crawl. . . . 'I don't want to know anything of
the ceremonies used when approaching Mr. Kurtz,' I
shouted. Curious, this feeling that came over me that
such details would be more intolerable than those
heads drying on the stakes under Mr. Kurtz's windows. After all, that was only a savage sight, while I
seemed at one bound to have been transported into

some lightless region of subtle horrors, where pure, uncomplicated savagery was a positive relief, being something that had a right to exist—obviously—in the sunshine. The young man looked at me with surprise. I suppose it did not occur to him that Mr. Kurtz was no idol of mine. He forgot I hadn't heard any of these splendid monologues on, what was it? on love, justice, conduct of life—or what not. If it had come to crawling before Mr. Kurtz, he crawled as much as the veriest savage of them all. I had no idea of the conditions, he said: these heads were the heads of rebels. I shocked him excessively by laughing. Rebels! What would be the next definition I was to hear? There had been enemies, criminals, workers—and these were rebels. Those rebellious heads looked very subdued to me on their sticks. 'You don't know how such a life tires a man like Kurtz,' cried Kurtz's last disciple. 'Well, and you?' I said. 'I! I! I am a simple man. I have no great thoughts. I want nothing from anybody. How can you compare me to . . . ?' His feelings were too much for speech, and suddenly he broke down. 'I don't understand,' he groaned. 'I've been doing my best to keep him alive, and that's enough. I had no hand in all this. I have no abilities. There hasn't been a drop of medicine or a mouthful of invalid food for months here. He was shamefully abandoned. A man like this, with such ideas. Shamefully! Shamefully! I— I—haven't slept for the last ten nights . . .'

"His voice lost itself in the calm of the evening. The long shadows of the forest had slipped downhill while we talked, had gone far beyond the ruined hovel, beyond the symbolic row of stakes. All this was in the gloom, while we down there were yet in the sunshine, and the stretch of the river abreast of the clearing glittered in a still and dazzling splendour, with a murky and overshadowed bend above and below. Not a living soul was seen on the shore. The bushes did not rustle.

"Suddenly round the corner of the house a group of men appeared, as though they had come up from the ground. They waded waist-deep in the grass, in a compact body, bearing an improvised stretcher in their midst. Instantly, in the emptiness of the landscape, a cry arose whose shrillness pierced the still air like a sharp arrow flying straight to the very heart of the land; and, as if by enchantment, streams of human beings—of naked human beings—with spears in their hands, with bows, with shields, with wild glances and savage movements, were poured into the clearing by the dark-faced and pensive forest. The bushes shook, the grass swayed for a time, and then everything stood still in attentive immobility.

" 'Now, if he does not say the right thing to them we are all done for,' said the Russian at my elbow. The knot of men with the stretcher had stopped, too, halfway to the steamer, as if petrified. I saw the man on the stretcher sit up, lank and with an uplifted arm, above the shoulders of the bearers. 'Let us hope that the man who can talk so well of love in general will find some particular reason to spare us this time,' I said. I resented bitterly the absurd danger of our situation, as if to be at the mercy of that atrocious phantom had been a dishonouring necessity. I could not hear a sound, but through my glasses I saw the thin arm extended commandingly, the lower jaw moving, the eyes of that apparition shining darkly far in its bony head that nodded with grotesque jerks. Kurtz—Kurtz—that means short in German—don't it? Well, the name was as true as everything else in life—and death. He looked at least seven feet long. His covering had fallen off, and his body emerged from it pitiful and appalling as from a winding-sheet. I could see the cage of his ribs all astir, the bones of his arm waving. It was as though an animated image of death carved out of old ivory had been shaking its hand with menaces at a motionless crowd of men made of dark and glittering bronze. I saw him open his mouth wide—it gave him a weirdly voracious aspect, as though he had wanted to swallow all the air, all the earth, all the men before him. A deep voice reached me faintly. He must have been shouting. He fell back suddenly. The stretcher shook as the bearers staggered forward again, and almost at the same time I noticed that the crowd of savages was vanishing without any perceptible movement of retreat, as if the forest that had ejected these beings so suddenly had drawn them in again as the breath is drawn in a long aspiration.

"Some of the pilgrims behind the stretcher carried his arms—two shot-guns, a heavy rifle, and a light revolver-carbine—the thunderbolts of that pitiful Jupiter. The manager bent over him murmuring as he walked beside his head. They laid him down in one of the little cabins—just a room for a bed place and a camp-stool or two, you know. We had brought his belated correspondence, and a lot of torn envelopes and open letters littered his bed. His hand roamed feebly amongst these papers. I was struck by the fire of his eyes and the composed languor of his expression. It was not so much the exhaustion of disease. He did not seem in pain. This shadow looked satiated and calm, as though for the moment it had had its fill of all the emotions.

"He rustled one of the letters, and looking straight in my face said, 'I am glad.' Somebody had been writing to him about me. These special recommendations were turning up again. The volume of tone he emitted without effort, almost without the trouble of moving his lips, amazed me. A voice! a voice! It was grave, profound, vibrating, while the man did not seem capable of a whisper. However, he had enough strength in him—factitious no doubt—to very nearly make an end of us, as you shall hear directly.

"The manager appeared silently in the doorway; I stepped out at once and he drew the curtain after me. The Russian, eyed curiously by the pilgrims, was staring at the shore. I followed the direction of his glance.

"Dark human shapes could be made out in the distance, flitting indistinctly against the gloomy border of the forest, and near the river two bronze figures, leaning on tall spears, stood in the sunlight under fantastic head-dresses of spotted skins, warlike and still in statuesque repose. And from right to left along the lighted shore moved a wild and gorgeous apparition of a woman.

"She walked with measured steps, draped in striped and fringed cloths, treading the earth proudly, with a slight jingle and flash of barbarous ornaments. She carried her head high; her hair was done in the shape of a helmet; she had brass leggings to the knee, brass wire gauntlets to the elbow, a crimson spot on her tawny cheek, innumerable necklaces of glass beads on her neck; bizarre things, charms, gifts of witch-men, that hung about her, glittered and trembled at every step. She must have had the value of several elephant tusks upon her. She was savage and superb, wild-eyed and magnificent; there was something ominous and stately in her deliberate progress. And in the hush that had fallen suddenly upon the whole sorrowful land, the immense wilderness, the colossal body of the fecund and mysterious life seemed to look at her, pensive, as though it had been looking at the image of its own tenebrous and passionate soul.

"She came abreast of the steamer, stood still, and faced us. Her long shadow fell to the water's edge. Her face had a tragic and fierce aspect of wild sorrow and of dumb pain mingled with the fear of some struggling, half-shaped resolve. She stood looking at us without a stir, and like the wilderness itself, with an air of brooding over an inscrutable purpose. A whole minute passed, and then she made a step forward. There was a low jingle, a glint of yellow metal, a sway of fringed draperies, and she stopped as if her heart had failed her. The young fellow by my side growled. The pilgrims murmured at my back. She looked at us all as if her life had depended upon the unswerving steadiness of her glance. Suddenly she opened her bared arms and threw them up rigid above her head, as though in an uncontrollable desire to touch the sky, and at the same time the swift shadows darted out on the earth, swept around on the river, gathering the steamer into a shadowy embrace. A formidable silence hung over the scene.

"She turned away slowly, walked on, following the

bank, and passed into the bushes to the left. Once only her eyes gleamed back at us in the dusk of the thickets before she disappeared.

" 'If she had offered to come aboard I really think I would have tried to shoot her,' said the man of patches, nervously. 'I have been risking my life every day for the last fortnight to keep her out of the house. She got in one day and kicked up a row about those miserable rags I picked up in the storeroom to mend my clothes with. I wasn't decent. At least it must have been that, for she talked like a fury to Kurtz for an hour, pointing at me now and then. I don't understand the dialect of this tribe. Luckily for me, I fancy Kurtz felt too ill that day to care, or there would have been mischief. I don't understand. . . . No—it's too much for me. Ah, well, it's all over now.'

"At this moment I heard Kurtz's deep voice behind the curtain: 'Save me!—save the ivory, you mean. Don't tell me. Save *me*! Why, I've had to save you. You are interrupting my plans now. Sick! Sick! Not so sick as you would like to believe. Never mind. I'll carry my ideas out yet—I will return. I'll show you what can be done. You with your little peddling notices—you are interfering with me. I will return. I. . . .' "

"The manager came out. He did me the honour to take me under the arm and lead me aside. 'He is very low, very low,' he said. He considered it necessary to sigh, but neglected to be consistently sorrowful. 'We have done all we could for him—haven't we? But there is no disguising the fact, Mr. Kurtz has done more harm than good to the Company. He did not see the time was not ripe for vigorous action. Cautiously, cautiously—that's my principle. We must be cautious yet. The district is closed to us for a time. Deplorable! Upon the whole, the trade will suffer. I don't deny there is a remarkable quantity of ivory—mostly fossil. We must save it, at all events—but look how precarious the position is—and why? Because the method is unsound.' 'Do you,' said I, looking at the shore, 'call it "unsound method?" ' 'Without doubt,' he exclaimed hotly. 'Don't you?' . . . 'No method at all,' I murmured after a while. 'Exactly,' he exulted. 'I anticipated this. Shows a complete want of judgment. It is my duty to point it out in the proper quarter.' 'Oh,' said I, 'that fellow—what's his name?—the brickmaker, will make a readable report for you.' He appeared confounded for a moment. It seemed to me I had never breathed an atmosphere so vile, and I turned mentally to Kurtz for relief—positively for relief. 'Nevertheless I think Mr. Kurtz is a remarkable man,' I said with emphasis. He started, dropped on me a cold heavy glance, said very quietly, 'he *was*,' and turned his back on me. My hour of favour was over; I found myself lumped along with Kurtz as a partisan of methods for which the time was not ripe: I was unsound! Ah! but it was something to have at least a choice of nightmares.

"I had turned to the wilderness really, not to Mr. Kurtz, who, I was ready to admit, was as good as buried. And for a moment it seemed to me as if I also were buried in a vast grave full of unspeakable secrets. I felt an intolerable weight oppressing my breast, the smell of the damp earth, the unseen presence of victorious corruption, the darkness of an impenetrable night. . . . The Russian tapped me on the shoulder. I heard him mumbling and stammering something about 'brother seaman—couldn't conceal—knowledge of matters that would affect Mr. Kurtz's reputation.' I waited. For him evidently Mr. Kurtz was not in his grave; I suspect that for him Mr. Kurtz was one of the immortals. "Well!" said I at last, 'speak out. As it happens, I am Mr. Kurtz's friend—in a way.'

"He stated with a good deal of formality that had we not been 'of the same profession,' he would have kept the matter to himself without regard to consequences. 'He suspected there was an active ill-will towards him on the part of these white men that—' 'You are right,' I said, remembering a certain conversation I had overheard. 'The manager thinks you ought to be hanged.' He showed a concern at this intelligence which amused me at first. 'I had better get out of the way quietly,' he said earnestly. 'I can do no more for Kurtz now, and they would soon find some excuse.

What's to stop them? There's a military post three hundred miles from here.' 'Well, upon my word,' said I, 'perhaps you had better go if you have any friends amongst the savages near by.' 'Plenty,' he said. 'They are simple people—and I want nothing, you know.' He stood biting his lip, then: 'I don't want any harm to happen to these whites here, but of course I was thinking of Mr. Kurtz's reputation—but you are a brother seaman and—' 'All right,' said I, after a time. 'Mr. Kurtz's reputation is safe with me.' I did not know how truly I spoke.

"He informed me, lowering his voice, that it was Kurtz who had ordered the attack to be made on the steamer. 'He hated sometimes the idea of being taken away—and then again. . . . But I don't understand these matters. I am a simple man. He thought it would scare you away—that you would give it up, thinking him dead. I could not stop him. Oh, I had an awful time of it this last month.' 'Very well,' I said. 'He is all right now.' 'Ye-e-es,' he muttered, not very convinced apparently. 'Thanks,' said I; 'I shall keep my eyes open.' 'Be quiet—eh?' he urged anxiously. 'It would be awful for his reputation if anybody here——' I promised a complete discretion with great gravity. 'I have a canoe and three black fellows waiting not very far. I am off. Could you give me a few Martini-Henry cartridges?' I could, and did, with proper secrecy. He helped himself, with a wink at me, to a handful of my tobacco.' 'Between sailors—you know—good English tobacco.' At the door of the pilot-house he turned round—'I say, haven't you a pair of shoes you could spare?' He raised one leg. 'Look.' The soles were tied with knotted strings sandalwise under his bare feet. I rooted out an old pair, at which he looked with admiration before tucking it under his left arm. One of his pockets (bright red) was bulging with cartridges, from the other (dark blue) peeped 'Towson's Inquiry,' etc., etc. He seemed to think himself excellently well equipped for a renewed encounter with the wilderness. 'Ah! I'll never, never meet such a man again. You ought to have heard him recite poetry—his own, too, it was, he told me. Poetry!' He rolled his eyes at the recollection of these delights. 'Oh, he enlarged my mind!' 'Good-bye,' said I. He shook hands and vanished in the night. Sometimes I ask myself whether I had ever really seen him—whether it was possible to meet such a phenomenon! . . .

"When I woke up shortly after midnight his warning came to my mind with its hint of danger that seemed, in the starred darkness, real enough to make me get up for the purpose of having a look round. On the hill a big fire burned, illuminating fitfully a crooked corner of the station-house. One of the agents with a picket of a few of our blacks, armed for the purpose, was keeping guard over the ivory; but deep within the forest, red gleams that wavered, that seemed to sink and rise from the ground amongst confused columnar shapes of intense blackness, showed the exact position of the camp where Mr. Kurtz's adorers were keeping their uneasy vigil. The monotonous beating of a big drum filled the air with muffled shocks and a lingering vibration. A steady droning sound of many men chanting each to himself some weird incantation came out from the black, flat wall of the woods as the humming of bees comes out of a hive, and had a strange narcotic effect upon my half-awake senses. I believe I dozed off leaning over the rail, till an abrupt burst of yells, an overwhelming outbreak of a pent-up and mysterious frenzy, woke me up in a bewildered wonder. It was cut short all at once, and the low droning went on with an effect of audible and soothing silence. I glanced casually into the little cabin. A light was burning within, but Mr. Kurtz was not there.

"I think I would have raised an outcry if I had believed my eyes. But I didn't believe them at first—the thing seemed so impossible. The fact is I was completely unnerved by a sheer blank fright, pure abstract terror, unconnected with any distinct shape of physical danger. What made this emotion so overpowering was—how shall I define it?—the moral shock I received, as if something altogether monstrous, intolerable to thought and odious to the soul, had been thrust upon me unexpectedly. This lasted of course the merest fraction of a second, and then the usual sense of commonplace, deadly danger, the possibility of a sudden onslaught and massacre, or something of the kind, which I saw impending, was positively welcome and composing. It pacified me, in fact, so much that I did not raise an alarm.

"There was an agent buttoned up inside an ulster and sleeping on a chair on deck within three feet of me. The yells had not awakened him; he snored very slightly; I left him to his slumbers and leaped ashore. I did not betray Mr. Kurtz—it was ordered I should never betray him—it was written I should be loyal to the nightmare of my choice. I was anxious to deal with this shadow by myself alone—and to this day I don't know why I was so jealous of sharing with any one the peculiar blackness of that experience.

"As soon as I got on the bank I saw a trail—a broad trail through the grass. I remember the exultation with which I said to myself, 'He can't walk—he is crawling on all-fours—I've got him.' The grass was wet with dew. I strode rapidly with clenched fists. I fancy I had some vague notion of falling upon him and giving him a drubbing. I don't know. I had some imbecile thoughts. The knitting old woman with the cat obtruded herself upon my memory as a most improper person to be sitting at the other end of such an affair. I saw a row of pilgrims squirting lead in the air out of Winchesters held to the hip. I thought I would never get back to the steamer, and imagined myself living alone and unarmed in the woods to an advanced age. Such silly things—you know. And I remember I confounded the beat of the drum with the beating of my heart, and was pleased at its calm regularity.

"I kept to the track though—then stopped to listen. The night was very clear; a dark blue space, sparkling with dew and starlight, in which black things stood very still. I thought I could see a kind of motion ahead of me. I was strangely cocksure of everything that night. I actually left the track and ran in a wide semi-circle (I verily believe chuckling to myself) so as to get in front of that stir, of that motion I had seen—if indeed I had seen anything. I was circumventing Kurtz as though it had been a boyish game.

"I came upon him, and if he had not heard me coming, I would have fallen over him, too, but he got up in time. He rose, unsteady, long, pale, indistinct, like a vapour exhaled by the earth, and swayed slightly, misty and silent before me; while at my back the fires loomed between the trees, and the murmur of many voices issued from the forest. I had cut him off cleverly; but when actually confronting him I seemed to come to my senses, I saw the danger in its right proportion. It was by no means over yet. Suppose he began to shout? Though he could hardly stand, there was still plenty of vigour in his voice. 'Go away—hide yourself,' he said, in that profound tone. It was very awful. I glanced back. We were within thirty yards from the nearest fire. A black figure stood up, strode on long black legs, waving long black arms, across the glow. It had horns—antelope horns, I think—on its head. Some sorcerer, some witch-man, no doubt: it looked fiendlike enough. 'Do you know what you are doing?' I whispered. 'Perfectly,' he answered, raising his voice for that single word: it sounded to me far off and yet loud, like a hail through a speaking-trumpet. 'If he makes a row we are lost,' I thought to myself. This clearly was not a case for fisticuffs, even apart from the very natural aversion I had to beat that Shadow—this wandering and tormented thing. 'You will be lost,' I said—'utterly lost.' One gets sometimes such a flash of inspiration, you know. I did say the right thing, though indeed he could not have been more irretrievably lost than he was at this very moment, when the foundations of our intimacy were being laid—to endure—to endure—even to the end—even beyond.

" 'I had immense plans,' he muttered irresolutely. 'Yes,' said I; 'but if you try to shout I'll smash your head with——' There was not a stick or a stone near. 'I will throttle you for good,' I corrected myself. 'I was on the threshold of great things,' he pleaded, in a voice

of longing, with a wistfulness of tone that made my
blood run cold. 'And now for this stupid scoundrel——'
'Your success in Europe is assured in any case,' I affirmed steadily. I did not want to have the throttling
of him, you understand and indeed it would have
been very little use for any practical purpose. I tried
to break the spell—the heavy, mute spell of the wilderness—that seemed to draw him to its pitiless breast
by the awakening of forgotten and brutal instincts, by
the memory of gratified and monstrous passions. This
alone, I was convinced, had driven him out to the edge
of the forest, to the bush, towards the gleam of fires,
the throb of drums, the drone of weird incantations;
this alone had beguiled his unlawful soul beyond the
bounds of permitted aspirations. And, don't you see,
the terror of the position was not in being knocked
on the head—though I had a very lively sense of that
danger, too—but in this, that I had to deal with a
being to whom I could not appeal in the name of
anything high or low. I had, even like the niggers, to
invoke him—himself—his own exalted and incredible
degradation. There was nothing either above or below
him, and I knew it. He had kicked himself loose of
the earth. Confound the man! he had kicked the very
earth to pieces. He was alone, and I before him did
not know whether I stood on the ground or floated in
the air. I've been telling you what we said—repeating
the phrases we pronounced—but what's the good?
They were common everyday words—the familiar,
vague sounds exchanged on every waking day of life.
But what of that? They had behind them, to my mind,
the terrific suggestiveness of words heard in dreams, of
phrases spoken in nightmares. Soul! If anybody ever
struggled with a soul, I am the man. And I wasn't
arguing with a lunatic either. Believe me or not, his
intelligence was perfectly clear—concentrated, it is
true, upon himself with horrible intensity, yet clear;
and therein was my only chance—barring, of course,
the killing him there and then, which wasn't so good,
on account of unavoidable noise. But his soul was
mad. Being alone in the wilderness, it had looked

within itself, and, by heavens! I tell you, it had gone mad. I had—for my sins, I suppose—to go through the ordeal of looking into it myself. No eloquence could have been so withering to one's belief in mankind as his final burst of sincerity. He struggled with himself, too. I saw it—I heard it. I saw the inconceivable mystery of a soul that knew no restraint, no faith, and no fear, yet struggling blindly with itself. I kept my head pretty well; but when I had him at last stretched on the couch, I wiped my forehead, while my legs shook under me as though I had carried half a ton on my back down that hill. And yet I had only supported him, his bony arm clasped round my neck—and he was not much heavier than a child.

"When next day we left at noon, the crowd, of whose presence behind the curtain of trees I had been acutely conscious all the time, flowed out of the woods again, filled the clearing, covered the slope with a mass of naked, breathing, quivering, bronze bodies. I steamed up a bit, then swung down stream, and two thousand eyes followed the evolutions of the splashing, thumping, fierce river-demon beating the water with its terrible tail and breathing black smoke into the air. In front of the first rank, along the river, three men, plastered with bright red earth from head to foot, strutted to and fro restlessly. When we came abreast again, they faced the river, stamped their feet, nodded their horned heads, swayed their scarlet bodies; they shook towards the fierce river-demon a bunch of black feathers, a mangy skin with a pendent tail—something that looked like a dried gourd; they shouted periodically together strings of amazing words that resembled no sounds of human language; and the deep murmurs of the crowd, interrupted suddenly, were like the responses of some satanic litany.

"We had carried Kurtz into the pilot-house: there was more air there. Lying on the couch, he stared through the open shutter. There was an eddy in the mass of human bodies, and the woman with helmeted head and tawny cheeks rushed out to the very brink of the stream. She put out her hands, shouted something, and all that wild mob took up the shout in a roaring chorus of articulated, rapid, breathless utterance.

" 'Do you understand this?' I asked.

"He kept on looking out past me with fiery, longing eyes, with a mingled expression of wistfulness and hate. He made no answer, but I saw a smile, a smile of indefinable meaning, appear on his colourless lips that a moment after twitched convulsively. 'Do I not?' he said slowly, gasping, as if the words had been torn out of him by a supernatural power.

"I pulled the string of the whistle, and I did this because I saw the pilgrims on deck getting out their rifles with an air of anticipating a jolly lark. At the sudden screech there was a movement of abject terror through that wedged mass of bodies. 'Don't! don't you frighten them away,' cried some one on deck disconsolately. I pulled the string time after time. They broke and ran, they leaped, they crouched, they swerved, they dodged the flying terror of the sound. The three red chaps had fallen flat, face down on the shore, as though they had been shot dead. Only the barbarous and superb woman did not so much as flinch, and stretched tragically her bare arms after us over the sombre and glittering river.

"And then that imbecile crowd down on the deck started their little fun, and I could see nothing more for smoke.

"The brown current ran swiftly out of the heart of darkness, bearing us down towards the sea with twice the speed of our upward progress; and Kurtz's life was running swiftly, too, ebbing, ebbing out of his heart into the sea of inexorable time. The manager was very placid, he had no vital anxieties now, he took us both in with a comprehensive and satisfied glance: the 'affair' had come off as well as could be wished. I saw the time approaching when I would be left alone of the party of 'unsound method.' The pilgrims looked upon me with disfavour. I was, so to speak, numbered with the dead. It is strange how I accepted this unforeseen partnership, this choice of nightmares forced upon me in the tenebrous land invaded by these mean and greedy phantoms.

"Kurtz discoursed. A voice! a voice! It rang deep to the very last. It survived his strength to hide in the magnificent folds of eloquence the barren darkness of his heart. Oh, he struggled! he struggled! The wastes of his weary brain were haunted by shadowy images now—images of wealth and fame revolving obsequiously round his unextinguishable gift of noble and lofty expression. My Intended, my station, my career, my ideas—these were the subjects for the occasional utterances of elevated sentiments. The shade of the original Kurtz frequented the bedside of the hollow sham, whose fate it was to be buried presently in the mould of primeval earth. But both the diabolic love and the unearthly hate of the mysteries it had penetrated fought for the possession of that soul satiated with primitive emotions, avid of lying fame, of sham distinction, of all the appearances of success and power.

"Sometimes he was contemptibly childish. He desired to have kings meet him at railway-stations on his return from some ghastly Nowhere, where he intended to accomplish great things. 'You show them you have in you something that is really profitable, and then there will be no limits to the recognition of your ability,' he would say. 'Of course you must take care of the motives—right motives—always.' The long reaches that were like one and the same reach, monotonous bends that were exactly alike, slipped past the steamer with their multitude of secular trees looking patiently after this grimy fragment of another world, the forerunner of change, of conquest, of trade, of massacres, of blessings. I looked ahead—piloting. 'Close the shutter,' said Kurtz suddenly one day; 'I can't bear to look at this.' I did so. There was a silence. 'Oh, but I will wring your heart yet!' he cried at the invisible wilderness.

"We broke down—as I had expected—and had to lie up for repairs at the head of an island. This delay was the first thing that shook Kurtz's confidence. One morning he gave me a packet of papers and a photograph—the lot tied together with a shoe-string. 'Keep this for me,' he said. 'This noxious fool' (meaning the manager) 'is capable of prying into my boxes when I am not looking.' In the afternoon I saw him. He was lying on his back with closed eyes, and I withdrew quietly, but I heard him mutter, 'Live rightly, die, die . . .' I listened. There was nothing more. Was he rehearsing some speech in his sleep, or was it a fragment of a phrase from some newspaper article? He had been writing for the papers and meant to do so again, 'for the furthering of my ideas. It's a duty.'

"His was an impenetrable darkness. I looked at him as you peer down at a man who is lying at the bottom of a precipice where the sun never shines. But I had not much time to give him, because I was helping the engine-driver to take to pieces the leaky cylinders, to straighten a bent connecting-rod, and in other such matters. I lived in an infernal mess of rust, filings, nuts, bolts, spanners, hammers, ratchet-drills—things I abominate, because I don't get on with them. I tended the little forge we fortunately had aboard; I toiled wearily in a wretched scrap-heap—unless I had the shakes too bad to stand.

"One evening coming in with a candle I was startled to hear him say a little tremulously, 'I am lying here in the dark waiting for death.' The light was within a foot of his eyes. I forced myself to murmur, 'Oh, nonsense!' and stood over him as if transfixed.

"Anything approaching the change that came over his features I have never seen before, and hope never to see again. Oh, I wasn't touched. I was fascinated. It was as though a veil had been rent. I saw on that ivory face the expression of sombre pride, of ruthless power, of craven terror—of an intense and hopeless despair. Did he live his life again in every detail of desire, temptation, and surrender during that supreme moment of complete knowledge? He cried in a whisper at some image, at some vision—he cried out twice, a cry that was no more than a breath:

" 'The horror! The horror!'

"I blew the candle out and left the cabin. The pilgrims were dining in the mess-room, and I took my place opposite the manager, who lifted his eyes to give me a questioning glance, which I successfully ignored. He leaned back, serene, with that peculiar smile of his sealing the unexpressed depths of his meanness. A continuous shower of small flies streamed upon the lamp, upon the cloth, upon our hands and faces. Suddenly the manager's boy put his insolent black head in the doorway, and said in a tone of scathing contempt:

" 'Mistah Kurtz—he dead.'

"All the pilgrims rushed out to see. I remained, and went on with my dinner. I believe I was considered brutally callous. However, I did not eat much. There was a lamp in there—light, don't you know—and outside it was so beastly, beastly dark. I went no more near the remarkable man who had pronounced a judgment upon the adventures of his soul on this earth. The voice was gone. What else had been there? But I am of course aware that next day the pilgrims buried something in a muddy hole.

"And then they very nearly buried me.

"However, as you see, I did not go to join Kurtz there and then. I did not. I remained to dream the nightmare out to the end, and to show my loyalty to Kurtz once more. Destiny. My destiny! Droll thing life is—that mysterious arrangement of merciless logic for a futile purpose. The most you can hope from it is some knowledge of yourself—that comes too late—a crop of unextinguishable regrets. I have wrestled with death. It is the most unexciting contest you can imagine. It takes place in an impalpable greyness, with nothing underfoot, with nothing around, without spectators, without clamour, without glory, without the great desire of victory, without the great fear of defeat, in a sickly atmosphere of tepid skepticism, without much belief in your own right, and still less in that of your adversary. If such is the form of ultimate wisdom, then life is a greater riddle than some of us think it to be. I was within a hair's breadth of the last opportunity of pronouncement, and I found with humiliation that probably I would have nothing to say. This is the reason why I affirm that Kurtz was a re-markable man. He had something to say. He said it. Since I had peeped over the edge myself, I understand better the meaning of his stare, that could not see the flame of the candle, but was wide enough to embrace the whole universe, piercing enough to penetrate all the hearts that beat in the darkness. He had summed up—he had judged. 'The horror!' He was a remark-able man. After all, this was the expression of some sort of belief; it had candour, it had conviction, it had a vibrating note of revolt in its whisper, it had the appalling face of a glimpsed truth—the strange com-mingling of desire and hate. And it is not my own extremity I remember best—a vision of greyness with-out form filled with physical pain, and a careless con-tempt for the evanescence of all things—even of this pain itself. No! It is his extremity that I seem to have lived through. True, he had made that last stride, he had stepped over the edge, while I had been permitted to draw back my hesitating foot. And perhaps in this is the whole difference; perhaps all the wisdom, and all truth, and all sincerity, are just compressed into that inappreciable moment of time in which we step over the threshold of the invisible. Perhaps! I like to think my summing-up would not have been a word of careless contempt. Better his cry—much better. It was an affirmation, a moral victory paid for by innumera-ble satisfactions. But it was a victory! That is why I have remained loyal to Kurtz to the last, and even beyond, when a long time after I heard once more, not his own voice, but the echo of his magnificent eloquence thrown to me from a soul as translucently pure as a cliff of crystal.

"No, they did not bury me, though there is a period of time which I remember mistily, with a shuddering wonder, like a passage through some inconceivable world that had no hope in it and no desire. I found myself back in the sepulchral city resenting the sight of people hurrying through the streets to filch a little

money from each other, to devour their infamous
cookery, to gulp their unwholesome beer, to dream
their insignificant and silly dreams. They trespassed
upon my thoughts. They were intruders whose knowledge of life was to me an irritating pretence, because
I felt so sure they could not possibly know the things
I knew. Their bearing, which was simply the bearing
of commonplace individuals going about their business
in the assurance of perfect safety, was offensive to me
like the outrageous flauntings of folly in the face of a
danger it is unable to comprehend. I had no particular
desire to enlighten them, but I had some difficulty in
restraining myself from laughing in their faces so full
of stupid importance. I daresay I was not very well at
that time. I tottered about the streets—there were various affairs to settle—grinning bitterly at perfectly respectable persons. I admit my behaviour was
inexcusable, but then my temperature was seldom normal in these days. My dear aunt's endeavours to 'nurse
up my strength' seemed altogether beside the mark.
It was not my strength that wanted nursing, it was my
imagination that wanted soothing. I kept the bundle
of papers given me by Kurtz, not knowing exactly
what to do with it. His mother had died lately,
watched over, as I was told, by his Intended. A clean-
shaved man, with an official manner and wearing gold-
rimmed spectacles, called on me one day and made
inquiries, at first circuitous, afterwards suavely pressing, about what he was pleased to denominate certain
'documents.' I was not surprised, because I had had
two rows with the manager on the subject out there.
I had refused to give up the smallest scrap out of
that package, and I took the same attitude with the
spectacled man. He became darkly menacing at last,
and with much heat argued that the Company had the
right to every bit of information about its 'territories.'
And said he, 'Mr. Kurtz's knowledge of unexplored
regions must have been necessarily extensive and peculiar—owing to his great abilities and to the deplorable circumstances in which he had been placed:
therefore——' I assured him Mr. Kurtz's knowledge,

however extensive, did not bear upon the problems of commerce or administration. He invoked then the name of science. 'It would be an incalculable loss if,' etc., etc. I offered him the report on the 'Suppression of Savage Customs,' with the postscriptum torn off. He took it up eagerly, but ended by sniffing at it with an air of contempt. 'This is not what we had a right to expect,' he remarked. 'Expect nothing else,' I said. 'There are only private letters.' He withdrew upon some threat of legal proceedings, and I saw him no more; but another fellow, calling himself Kurtz's cousin, appeared two days later, and was anxious to hear all the details about his dear relative's last moments. Incidentally he gave me to understand that Kurtz had been essentially a great musician. 'There was the making of an immense success,' said the man, who was an organist, I believe, with lank grey hair flowing over a greasy coat-collar. I had no reason to doubt this statement; and to this day I am unable to say what was Kurtz's profession, whether he ever had any—which was the greatest of his talents. I had taken him for a painter who wrote for the papers, or else for a journalist who could paint—but even the cousin (who took snuff during the interview) could not tell me what he had been—exactly. He was a universal genius—on that point I agreed with the old chap, who thereupon blew his nose noisily into a large cotton handkerchief and withdrew in senile agitation, bearing off some family letters and memoranda without importance. Ultimately a journalist anxious to know something of the fate of his 'dear colleague' turned up. This visitor informed me Kurtz's proper sphere ought to have been politics 'on the popular side.' He had furry straight eyebrows, bristly hair cropped short, an eyeglass on a broad ribbon, and, becoming expansive, confessed his opinion that Kurtz really couldn't write a bit—'but heavens! how that man could talk. He electrified large meetings. He had faith—don't you see?—he had the faith. He could get himself to believe anything—anything. He would have been a splendid leader of an extreme party.' 'What party?' I asked.

'Any party,' answered the other. 'He was an—an—extremist.' Did I not think so? I assented. Did I know, he asked, with a sudden flash of curiosity, 'what it was that had induced him to go out there?' 'Yes,' said I, and forthwith handed him the famous Report for publication, if he thought fit. He glanced through it hurriedly, mumbling all the time, judged "it would do,' and took himself off with this plunder.

"Thus I was left at last with a slim packet of letters and the girl's portrait. She struck me as beautiful—I mean she had a beautiful expression. I know that the sunlight can be made to lie, too, yet one felt that no manipulation of light and pose could have conveyed the delicate shade of truthfulness upon those features. She seemed ready to listen without mental reservation, without suspicion, without a thought for herself. I concluded I would go and give her back her portrait and those letters myself. Curiosity? Yes; and also some other feeling perhaps. All that had been Kurtz's had passed out of my hands: his soul, his body, his station, his plans, his ivory, his career. There remained only his memory and his Intended—and I wanted to give that up, too, to the past, in a way—to surrender personally all that remained of him with me to that oblivion which is the last word of our common fate. I don't defend myself. I had no clear perception of what it was I really wanted. Perhaps it was an impulse of unconscious loyalty, or the fulfilment of one of those ironic necessities that lurk in the facts of human existence. I don't know. I can't tell. But I went.

"I thought his memory was like the other memories of the dead that accumulate in every man's life—a vague impress on the brain of shadows that had fallen on it in their swift and final passage; but before the high and ponderous door, between the tall houses of a street as still and decorous as a well-kept alley in a cemetery, I had a vision of him on the stretcher, opening his mouth voraciously, as if to devour all the earth with all its mankind. He lived then before me; he lived as much as he had ever lived—a shadow insatiable of

splendid appearances, of frightful realities; a shadow
darker than the shadow of the night, and draped nobly
in the folds of a gorgeous eloquence. The vision
seemed to enter the house with me—the stretcher, the
phantom-bearers, the wild crowd of obedient worship-
pers, the gloom of the forests, the glitter of the reach
between the murky bends, the beat of the drum, regular and muffled like the beating of a heart—the heart
of a conquering darkness. It was a moment of triumph
for the wilderness, an invading and vengeful rush
which, it seemed to me, I would have to keep back
alone for the salvation of another soul. And the memory of what I had heard him say afar there, with the
horned shapes stirring at my back, in the glow of fires,
within the patient woods, those broken phrases came
back to me, were heard again in their ominous and
terrifying simplicity. I remembered his abject pleading,
his abject threats, the colossal scale of his vile desires,
the meanness, the torment, the tempestuous anguish
of his soul. And later on I seemed to see his collected
languid manner, when he said one day, 'This lot of
ivory now is really mine. The Company did not pay
for it. I collected it myself at a very great personal
risk. I am afraid they will try to claim it as theirs
though. H'm. It is a difficult case. What do you think
I ought to do—resist? Eh? I want no more than
justice.' . . . He wanted no more than justice—no more
than justice. I rang the bell before a mahogany door
on the first floor, and while I waited he seemed to
stare at me out of the glassy panel—stare with that
wide and immense stare embracing, condemning,
loathing all the universe. I seemed to hear the whispered cry, 'The horror! The horror!'

"The dusk was falling. I had to wait in a lofty drawing-
room with three long windows from floor to ceiling
that were like three luminous and bedraped columns.
The bent gilt legs and backs of the furniture shone in
indistinct curves. The tall marble fireplace had a cold
and monumental whiteness. A grand piano stood mas-
sively in a corner; with dark gleams on the flat surfaces

like a sombre and polished sarcophagus. A high door opened—closed. I rose.

"She came forward, all in black, with a pale head, floating towards me in the dusk. She was in mourning. It was more than a year since his death, more than a year since the news came; she seemed as though she would remember and mourn forever. She took both my hands in hers and murmured, 'I had heard you were coming.' I noticed she was not very young—I mean not girlish. She had a mature capacity for fidelity, for belief, for suffering. The room seemed to have grown darker, as if all the sad light of the cloudy evening had taken refuge on her forehead. This fair hair, this pale visage, this pure brow, seemed surrounded by an ashy halo from which the dark eyes looked out at me. Their glance was guileless, profound, confident, and trustful. She carried her sorrowful head as though she were proud of that sorrow, as though she would say, 'I—I alone knew how to mourn for him as he deserves.' But while we were still shaking hands, such a look of awful desolation came upon her face that I perceived she was one of those creatures that are not the playthings of Time. For her he had died only yesterday. And, by Jove! the impression was so powerful that for me, too, he seemed to have died only yesterday—nay, this very minute. I saw her and him in the same instant of time—his death and her sorrow—I saw her sorrow in the very moment of his death. Do you understand? I saw them together—I heard them together. She had said, with a deep catch of the breath, 'I have survived' while my strained ears seemed to hear distinctly, mingled with her tone of despairing regret, the summing up whisper of his eternal condemnation. I asked myself what I was doing there, with a sensation of panic in my heart as though I had blundered into a place of cruel and absurd mysteries not fit for a human being to behold. She motioned me to a chair. We sat down. I laid the packet gently on the little table, and she put her hand over it. . . . 'You knew him well,' she murmured, after a moment of mourning silence.

" 'Intimacy grows quickly out there,' I said. 'I knew him as well as it is possible for one man to know another.'

" 'And you admired him,' she said. 'It was impossible to know him and not to admire him. Was it?'

" 'He was a remarkable man,' I said, unsteadily. Then before the appealing fixity of her gaze, that seemed to watch for more words on my lips, I went on, 'It was impossible not to——'

" 'Love him,' she finished eagerly, silencing me into an appalled dumbness. 'How true! how true! But when you think that no one knew him so well as I! I had all his noble confidence. I knew him best.'

" 'You knew him best,' I repeated. And perhaps she did. But with every word spoken the room was growing darker, and only her forehead, smooth and white, remained illumined by the unextinguishable light of belief and love.

" 'You were his friend,' she went on. 'His friend,' she repeated, a little louder. 'You must have been, if he had given you this, and sent you to me. I feel I can speak to you—and oh! I must speak. I want you—you who have heard his last words—to know I have been worthy of him. . . . It is not pride. . . . Yes! I am proud to know I understood him better than any one on earth—he told me so himself. And since his mother died I have had no one—no one—to—to—'

"I listened. The darkness deepened. I was not even sure whether he had given me the right bundle. I rather suspect he wanted me to take care of another batch of his papers which, after his death, I saw the manager examining under the lamp. And the girl talked, easing her pain in the certitude of my sympathy; she talked as thirsty men drink. I had heard that her engagement with Kurtz had been disapproved by her people. He wasn't rich enough or something. And indeed I don't know whether he had not been a pauper all his life. He had given me some reason to infer that it was his impatience of comparative poverty that drove him out there.

" '. . . Who was not his friend who had heard him

speak once?' she was saying. 'He drew men towards him by what was best in them.' She looked at me with intensity. 'It is the gift of the great,' she went on, and the sound of her low voice seemed to have the accompaniment of all the other sounds, full of mystery, desolation, and sorrow, I had ever heard—the ripple of the river, the soughing of the trees swayed by the wind, the murmurs of the crowds, the faint ring of incomprehensible words cried from afar, the whisper of a voice speaking from beyond the threshold of an eternal darkness. 'But you have heard him! You know!' she cried.

" 'Yes, I know,' I said with something like despair in my heart, but bowing my head before the faith that was in her, before that great and saving illusion that shone with an unearthly glow in the darkness, in the triumphant darkness from which I could not have defended her—from which I could not even defend myself.

" 'What a loss to me—to us!'—she corrected herself with beautiful generosity; then added in a murmur, 'To the world.' By the last gleams of twilight I could see the glitter of her eyes, full of tears—of tears that would not fall.

" 'I have been very happy—very fortunate—very proud,' she went on. 'Too fortunate. Too happy for a little while. And now I am unhappy for—for life.'

"She stood up; her fair hair seemed to catch all the remaining light in a glimmer of gold. I rose, too.

" 'And of all this,' she went on mournfully, 'of all his promise, and of all his greatness, of his generous mind, of his noble heart, nothing remains—nothing but a memory. You and I——'

" 'We shall always remember him,' I said hastily.

" 'No!' she cried. 'It is impossible that all this should be lost—that such a life should be sacrificed to leave nothing—but sorrow. You know what vast plans he had. I knew of them, too—I could not perhaps understand—but others knew of them. Something must remain. His words, at least, have not died.'

" 'His words will remain,' I said.

" 'And his example,' she whispered to herself. 'Men looked up to him—his goodness shone in every act. His example——'

" 'True,' I said; 'his example, too. Yes, his example. I forgot that.'

" 'But I do not. I cannot—I cannot believe—not yet. I cannot believe that I shall never see him again, that nobody will see him again, never, never, never.'

"She put out her arms as if after a retreating figure, stretching them back and with clasped pale hands across the fading and narrow sheen of the window. Never see him! I saw him clearly enough then. I shall see this eloquent phantom as long as I live, and I shall see her, too, a tragic and familiar Shade, resembling in this gesture another one, tragic also, and bedecked with powerless charms, stretching bare brown arms over the glitter of the infernal stream, the stream of darkness. She said suddenly very low, 'He died as he lived.'

" 'His end,' said I, with dull anger stirring in me, 'was in every way worthy of his life.'

" 'And I was not with him,' she murmured. My anger subsided before a feeling of infinite pity.

" 'Everything that could be done——' I mumbled.

" 'Ah, but I believed in him more than any one on earth—more than his own mother, more than—himself. He needed me! Me! I would have treasured every sigh, every word, every sign, every glance.'

"I felt like a chill grip on my chest. 'Don't,' I said, in a muffled voice.

" 'Forgive me. I—I have mourned so long in silence—in silence. . . . You were with him—to the last? I think of his loneliness. Nobody near to understand him as I would have understood. Perhaps no one to hear. . . .'

" 'To the very end,' I said, shakily. 'I heard his very last words. . . .' I stopped in a fright.

" 'Repeat them,' she murmured in a heart-broken tone. 'I want—I want—something—something—to—to live with.'

"I was on the point of crying at her, 'Don't you

hear them?' The dusk was repeating them in a persistent whisper all around us, in a whisper that seemed to swell menacingly like the first whisper of a rising wind. 'The horror! The horror!'

" 'His last word—to live with,' she insisted. 'Don't you understand I loved him—I loved him—I loved him!'

"I pulled myself together and spoke slowly.

" 'The last words he pronounced was—your name.'

"I heard a light sigh and then my heart stood still, stopped dead short by an exulting and terrible cry, by the cry of inconceivable triumph and of unspeakable pain. 'I knew it—I was sure!' . . . She knew. She was sure. I heard her weeping; she had hidden her face in her hands. It seemed to me that the house would collapse before I could escape, that the heavens would fall upon my head. But nothing happened. The heavens do not fall for such a trifle. Would they have fallen, I wonder, if I had rendered Kurtz that justice which was his due? Hadn't he said he wanted only justice? But I couldn't. I could not tell her. It would have been too dark—too dark altogether. . . ."

Marlow ceased, and sat apart, indistinct and silent, in the pose of a meditating Buddha. Nobody moved for a time. "We have lost the first of the ebb," said the Director suddenly. I raised my head. The offing was barred by a black bank of clouds, and the tranquil waterway leading to the uttermost ends of the earth flowed sombre under an overcast sky—seemed to lead into the heart of an immense darkness.

SELECTED BIBLIOGRAPHY

Works by Joseph Conrad

Almayer's Folly: A Story of an Eastern River, 1895 Novel

An Outcast of the Islands, 1896 Novel

The Nigger of the "Narcissus": A Tale of the Sea, 1897 Novel

Tales of Unrest ("Karain: A Memory," "The Idiots," An Outpost of Progress," "The Return," and "The Lagoon"), 1898 Short Stories

Lord Jim: A Tale, 1900 Novel (Signet Classic 0-451-522346)

The Inheritors: An Extravagant Story (with Ford Madox Hueffer), 1901 Novel

Youth: A Narrative; and Two Other Stories ("Youth," "Heart of Darkness," and "The End of the Tether"), 1902 Novel

Typhoon and Other Stories ("Typhoon," "Amy Foster," "Falk," and "To-morrow") 1903 Short Stories

Romance: A Novel, 1903 Novel

Nostromo: A Tale of the Seaboard, 1904 Novel

The Mirror of the Sea: Memories and Impressions, 1906 Travel Writings

The Secret Agent: A Simple Tale, 1907 Novel (Signet Classic 0-451-524160)

A Set of Six ("Gaspar Ruiz," "The Informer," "The Brute," "An Anarchist," "The Duel," and "Il Conde"), 1908 Short Stories

Under Western Eyes, 1911 Novel (Signet Classic 0-451-521145)

A Personal Record, 1912 Autobiography

'Twixt Land and Sea: Tales ("A Smile of Fortune," "The Secret Sharer," and "Freya of the Seven Isles"), 1912 Short Stories

Chance: A Tale in Two Parts, 1914 Novel (Signet Classic 0-451-525574)

Within the Tides ("The Planter of Malata," "The Part-

ner," "The Inn of the Two Witches," and "Because
of the Dollars"), 1915 Short Stories
Victory: An Island Tale, 1915 Novel (Signet Classic
0-451-525310)
The Shadow-Line, 1917 Novel
The Arrow of Gold: A Story Between Two Notes, 1919
Novel
Notes on Life and Letters, 1921 Memoir
The Rover, 1923 Novel
The Nature of a Crime (with Ford Madox Ford [né Huef-
fer]), 1924 Novel
Suspense: A Napoleonic Novel (incomplete), 1925 Novel
Tales of Hearsay ("The Warrior's Soul," "Prince
Roman," "The Tale," and "The Black Mate"), 1925
Short Stories
Last Essays, 1926 Essays
The Sisters (begun 1896, incomplete), 1928 Novel
*Three Plays: Laughing Anne, One Day More, and The
Secret Agent,* 1934 Plays
Congo Diary and Other Uncollected Pieces, 1978
Travel Writings

Criticism and Biography

Baines, Jocelyn. *Joseph Conrad: A Critical Biography.*
London: Weidenfeld & Nicolson; New York: McGraw-
Hill, 1960; reprinted Penguin, 1971
Batchelor, John. *The Life of Joseph Conrad: A Critical
Biography.* Oxford: Blackwell, 1994.
Berthoud, Jacques, *Joseph Conrad: The Major Phase.*
Cambridge; Cambridge University Press, 1978.
Billy, Ted, ed. *Critical Essays on Joseph Conrad.* Boston:
Hall, 1987.
Bloom, Harold, ed. *Joseph Conrad: Modern Critical
Views.* New York: Chelsea House, 1986.
Bode, Rita. " 'They . . . Should be Out of It': The
Women of *Heart of Darkness.*" *Conradiana: A Journal
of Joseph Conrad Studies* 26:1 (1994), 20–34.
Burden, Robert. *Heart of Darkness.* The Critics Debate
Series. Basingstoke: Macmillan, 1991.
Carabine, Keith, Owen Knowles, and Wieslaw Krajka,
eds. *Contexts for Conrad.* Boulder, Colo.: East Euro-
pean Monographs, 1993.

Conroy, Mark. *Modernism and Authority: Strategies of Legitimation in Flaubert and Conrad.* Baltimore: Johns Hopkins University Press, 1985.

Daleski, H. M. *Joseph Conrad: The Way of Dispossession.* London: Faber & Faber; New York: Holmes & Meier, 1977.

Eagleton, Terry. *Exiles and Emigrés.* London: Chatto & Windus, 1970.

Gillon, Adam. *Joseph Conrad.* Twayne English Authors No. 333. Boston: Twayne, 1982.

Gordan, John Dozier. *Joseph Conrad: The Making of a Novelist.* Cambridge, Mass.: Harvard University Press, 1940.

Hamner, Robert D., ed. *Joseph Conrad: Third World Perspectives.* Washington, D.C.: Three Continents, 1990.

Hawthorn, Jeremy. *Joseph Conrad: Language and Fictional Self-Consciousness.* London: Arnold; Lincoln: University of Nebraska Press, 1979.

———. *Joseph Conrad: Narrative Technique and Ideological Commitment.* London: Edward Arnold, 1990.

Henricksen, Bruce. *Nomadic Voices: Conrad and the Subject of Narrative.* Urbana: University of Illinois Press, 1992.

Jameson, Fredric. *The Political Unconscious: Narrative as a Socially Symbolic Act.* London: Methuen: Ithac, N.Y.: Cornell University Press, 1981.

Kimbrough, Robert, ed. *Heart of Darkness.* New York: Norton, 1988.

Leavis, F. R. "Revaluations: Joseph Conrad." *Scrutiny* 10:1 (1941), 22–50; and 10:2 (1941), 157–81. Reprinted in *The Great Tradition: George Eliot, Henry James, Joseph Conrad.* London: Chatto & Windus; New York: G. W. Stewart, 1948.

Moore, Gene, ed. *Conrad's Cities: Essays for Hans van Marle.* Amsterdam: Rodopi, 1992.

Murfin, Ross C., ed. *Joseph Conrad: Heart of Darkness.* Boston: St. Martin's, 1996.

Najder, Zdzislaw. *Joseph Conrad: A Chronicle.* Trans. Halina Carroll-Najder. New Brunswick, N.J.: Rutgers University Press; Cambridge: Cambridge University Press, 1983.

Parry, Benita. *Conrad and Imperialism: Ideological*

Boundaries and Visionary Frontiers. London: Macmillan; Topsfield, Mass.: Salem Academy/Merrimack, 1984.

Said, Edward W. *Joseph Conrad and the Fiction of Autobiography.* Cambridge, Mass.: Harvard University Press, 1966.

Sherry, Norman. *Conrad.* London: Thames & Hudson, 1972, reprinted 1988; New York: Scribner's, 1977. ·

———. *Conrad: The Critical Heritage.* London: Routledge & Kegan Paul, 1973.

Stape, J. H., ed. *The Cambridge Companion to Joseph Conrad.* Cambridge: Cambridge University Press, 1966.

Watt, Ian. *Conrad in the Nineteenth Century.* Berkeley: University of California Press, 1979; London: Chatto & Windus, 1980.

Watts, Cedric. *Joseph Conrad: A Literary Life.* London: Macmillan, 1989.

READ THE TOP 25 SIGNET CLASSICS

ANIMAL FARM BY GEORGE ORWELL   0-451-52634-1

1984 BY GEORGE ORWELL   0-451-52493-4

HAMLET BY WILLIAM SHAKESPEARE   0-451-52692-9

FRANKENSTEIN BY MARY SHELLEY   0-451-52771-2

THE SCARLET LETTER BY NATHANIEL HAWTHORNE   0-451-52608-2

THE ADVENTURES OF HUCKLEBERRY FINN BY MARK TWAIN   0-451-52650-3

THE ODYSSEY BY HOMER   0-451-52736-4

FRANKENSTEIN, DRACULA, DR. JEKYLL AND MR. HYDE
  BY MARY SHELLEY, BRAM STOKER, AND ROBERT LOUIS STEVENSON
                                                               0-451-52363-6

JANE EYRE BY CHARLOTTE BRONTE   0-451-52655-4

HEART OF DARKNESS & THE SECRET SHARER
  BY JOSEPH CONRAD   0-451-52657-0

GREAT EXPECTATIONS BY CHARLES DICKENS   0-451-52671-6

BEOWULF (BURTON RAFFEL, TRANSLATOR)   0-451-52740-2

ETHAN FROME BY EDITH WHARTON   0-451-52766-6

NARRATIVE OF THE LIFE OF FREDERICK DOUGLASS
  BY FREDERICK DOUGLASS   0-451-52673-2

A TALE OF TWO CITIES BY CHARLES DICKENS   0-451-52656-2

OTHELLO BY WILLIAM SHAKESPEARE   0-451-52685-6

ONE DAY IN THE LIFE OF IVAN DENISOVICH
  BY ALEXANDER SOLZHENITSYN   0-451-52709-7

PRIDE AND PREJUDICE BY JANE AUSTEN   0-451-52588-4

UNCLE TOM'S CABIN: 150TH ANNIVERSARY EDITION
  BY HARRIET BEECHER STOWE   0-451-52670-8

MACBETH BY WILLIAM SHAKESPEARE   0-451-52677-5

THE COUNT OF MONTE CRISTO BY ALEXANDER DUMAS   0-451-52195-1

ROMEO AND JULIET BY WILLIAM SHAKESPEARE   0-451-52686-4

A MIDSUMMER NIGHT'S DREAM BY WILLIAM SHAKESPEARE   0-451-52696-1

THE PRINCE BY NICCOLO MACHIAVELLI   0-451-52746-1

WUTHERING HEIGHTS BY EMILY BRONTE   0-451-52338-5